There was no way around it.

Ty had to lay it all on the line. "Well, there's me." He wanted, needed, to know if there was a future for them. "So, what do you think?"

"How about we take it one step at a time and see where the road leads?"

"Sounds like a plan," he agreed. Especially if that road led where he hoped it would.

He settled into the saddle, the pounding of his heart easing. Comfortable with the decision they'd made, he spent the next few minutes dreaming of what the future might hold for them. The idea of coming home to a house filled with love and laughter instead of silence and empty rooms deepened the smile on his lips.

He pictured Sarah standing on the wide front porch, a baby in her arms and Jimmy at her side.

Dear Reader,

When I was young, my dad frequently hitched the pop-up trailer to the station wagon and aimed for one of Florida's state parks. There, my folks relaxed while my sister and I swam or fished. We hunted buried treasure and toasted marshmallows. As I grew older, my interests shifted from pirates' gold to boys. My first kiss came on a camping trip and, along with it, my first dreams of falling in love.

Camping out plays a large role in *Rancher's Son* when fourth-generation cattleman Ty Parker looks into his childless future and asks what will become of the ranch he's worked to preserve. His answer might be a five-year-old boy abandoned on DCF's doorstep, but only if the cowboy can convince a jaded social worker he's good father material. When Sarah Magarity insists on accompanying Ty and the child on a cattle drive through Florida's version of the Old West, the fulfillment of all their dreams could be just around the next bend.

I loved writing *Rancher's Son,* and I'm especially grateful that Ty and Sarah's story gave me the chance to relive so many of my favorite childhood experiences. Special thanks go out to Roxanne St. Claire, Kristen Painter and the ever-encouraging Lara Santiago who kept the magic of Library Days flowing while I worked on this project.

I hope you enjoy reading *Rancher's Son* as much as I enjoyed writing it. I'd love to hear from you. Please visit me at www.leighduncan.com.

Leigh

Rancher's Son

LEIGH DUNCAN

HARLEQUIN®
entertain, enrich, inspire™

ISBN-13: 978-0-373-75435-9

RANCHER'S SON

This edition published by arrangement with Harlequin Books S.A.

For questions and comments about the quality of this book, please contact us at CustomerService@Harlequin.com.

www.Harlequin.com

Printed in U.S.A.

ABOUT THE AUTHOR

Award-winning author Leigh Duncan writes the kind of books she loves to read—ones where home, family and community are key to the happy endings we all deserve. Married to the love of her life and mother of two wonderful young adults, Leigh lives on central Florida's east coast.

When she isn't busy working on her next story for Harlequin American Romance, Leigh loves nothing better than to curl up in her favorite chair with a cup of hot coffee and a great book. She invites readers to follow her on Twitter or Facebook. Contact her at P.O. Box 410787, Melbourne, FL 32941, or visit her online at www.leighduncan.com.

Books by Leigh Duncan

HARLEQUIN AMERICAN ROMANCE

1304—THE OFFICER'S GIRL
1360—THE DADDY CATCH
1406—RODEO DAUGHTER

For

Cyndi & Matt and Bryan & Kristy.

The love you share is the inspiration behind my stories.

Chapter One

Sarah Magarity rose to her tiptoes on the stepladder. The large silver star atop the Christmas tree wobbled when her fingers brushed against it. As she wrestled the heavy ornament from the center post, it tipped, threatening to throw her off balance. For a second, Sarah saw herself lying on the floor, alone and injured, through the long holiday weekend. Normally hectic on a Thursday afternoon, the Department of Children and Family Services in Fort Pierce, Florida, had slowly emptied once the tech guys shut down the computers for a system-wide upgrade. Now only a tree that smelled more like plastic than pine stood between her and a much-needed two weeks out from under a crushing workload.

Two weeks of white, sandy beaches and a cell phone that didn't buzz with a new crisis every ten minutes. Two weeks of gathering plants for her growing collection of tropical flowers. Sarah took a deep breath and braced herself against the wall. She could almost smell Hawaiian orchids and plumeria.

Dreaming of ukuleles and fruity concoctions decorated with tiny umbrellas, she whistled a slightly off-key version of "Somewhere Over the Rainbow." Carefully, she toted the star down the ladder. Her foot had barely touched the worn carpet when one of the doors at the main entrance swung open. Sounds of heavy traffic on U.S. Highway 1 blared into the office before the door swished closed. Silence, broken only by the noisy hum of an air conditioner, once more filled the room.

"C'mon, Jimmy." A voice whined over the warren of empty cubicles. "We hav'ta find someone pronto. It's late."

Late for what?

Sarah swallowed a groan. Whoever had arrived at four-thirty on Christmas Eve, they were late, all right. The holiday party for kids in foster care had ended at two.

"Can I help you?" Sarah prayed the curvy brunette rounding the last of the partitions wanted nothing more than grocery money. A couple of ten-dollar gift cards, and not much else, remained in the emergency fund.

"This is Jimmy Parker." The woman's plunging neckline dipped perilously low as she placed her hand square on the back of the little boy at her side and shoved. The child stumbled forward. "His mom asked me to drop him off."

Sarah mustered a smile for the pair of sad brown eyes that peered up from beneath a thatch of sandy-blond hair. The boy's hollow gaze met hers only briefly before he looked away. When his focus dropped to a pair of tattered sneakers, Sarah hiked an eyebrow. She skimmed over high-water jeans, frowned at a shirt Goodwill would reject. Fighting a protective nature that made her want to wrap the little boy in her arms and make everything right in his world, Sarah stiffened her spine.

The brutal truth was, a dozen kids just like this

one walked into the DCF offices each month. She had a hundred more open cases in her file cabinet. She couldn't give every child assigned to her the attention they deserved. Not and still keep her sanity. The situation was far from her idealistic dream of how things ought to work. But there were too many at-risk kids, too few dollars to go around and too few workers to do the job.

Letting her eyes narrow, she faced the older of her guests head-on. "You're too late." She grimaced when a little more vehemence than usual crept into her voice. "The party was hours ago. You should have been here then."

Despite herself, Sarah glanced across the room at a whimsical mural of a sleigh propelled by eight flying porpoises. Were there any presents left? Not a chance. Every gift from Santa's bag had been distributed into the eager hands of other kids who were just as needy as this one.

"Party?" The latecomer's dark eyebrows lifted. "Who said anything about a party?" The brunette chewed a wad of gum and swallowed. "I promised to deliver the kid, and here he is."

An uneasy feeling settled in Sarah's chest when her visitor dropped a worn duffel bag to the floor.

"Hold on a sec," she ordered. "Maybe you'd better start at the beginning and tell me exactly what brought you here. I'm Sarah Magarity, the senior caseworker." She paused for a look around. With no husband or children of her own to rush home to, she'd offered to keep the office open until closing time. A skeleton staff would report in on Monday and man the offices through the New Year. For tonight, though, she was it. "And you are?"

"Candy. Candace, really, but everyone just calls me Candy." The woman settled one hand on a cocked hip. "Candy Storm. And this little guy," she said, tapping a bloodred fingernail on the boy's head, "is James Tyrone Parker. Jimmy. He's five. His mom was my best friend."

The implication sent Sarah's stomach into free fall. She swept another look at the child who studied the stained carpet at his feet. "His mom is…?"

"Yeah." Candy blinked several times before patting the skin beneath lashes so long they had to be fake.

"I think you and I should talk privately." Sarah motioned toward a nearby cubicle. "Jimmy, I need you to watch TV or play with some toys while Miss Candy and I chat for a few minutes."

Without waiting for a response, Sarah took the child's tiny hand in hers. His thin shoulders and bony frame raised troubling questions. When was the last time this kid ate? How long ago had his mother passed? Who had been taking care of him since then? And where?

Her tone softened. "I think we have some cookies in the break room. Would you like some?" When Jimmy didn't answer, she called to Candy. "Does he have any allergies?"

The woman's gum snapped and popped before she shrugged a vague "Nope?"

As the child scrambled onto the couch near the bare Christmas tree, Sarah overlooked his soiled shirt and grimy fingernails, knowing that if she accused the parents of every unwashed youngster of neglect, the foster system would collapse under the load. Bruises or injuries were another matter, and she scanned the child for visible signs. Her breath eased at the sight of pale, but unblemished, skin. Relieved that the boy wasn't in immediate physical danger—and thus, not really her problem—she clamped a heavy lid over the urge to take him under her wing.

She couldn't get involved. Not now. Not when doing so would ruin her plans for the holidays and dash her hope to rest and recharge. And, after five years with the DCF in Melbourne and two more in Fort Pierce, it was either that or quit. No, she shook her head, this little boy was Candy's problem and he had to stay that way. At least until next week when her coworkers would be back in the office. Steeling her heart, she settled him in front of a cartoon video with a small plate of cookies and a juice box she took from the office refrigerator.

"Okay, what's this all about?"

With Candy lagging behind, Sarah led the way to a cubicle where a line of red *X*'s across the bottom of the calendar marked the vacation days she had to use or lose according to DCF's policy manual. She waved her guest into the only other chair in the cramped space and swung to her computer. She stilled. Until the IT department completed their work, no one could access the DCF database. Or learn whether Jimmy Parker already had a caseworker to look after him.

With a sigh, Sarah pulled a yellow legal pad and a pen from a drawer and hoped Candy would quickly get to the point. Across the desk, the woman gave her a petulant look, her jaw jutting forward.

"Millie, Jimmy's mom, made me swear if anything ever happened to her, I'd bring the kid to Florida," she said, with an accent from considerably north of the Sunshine State. "She said his dad owns a ranch somewhere near Lake Okeechobee. Jimmy's named after him."

James Tyrone Parker.

Sarah pursed her lips at the memory of a tall, broad-shouldered rancher with sun-bleached hair. She brushed a speck of dust from the desktop, chasing the image away. Surely there were thousands of Parkers in the hundreds of square miles bordering the largest lake in Florida. There were probably a dozen Jims and Tys among them. The odds against this little boy's father being the same Ty Parker she'd run out of DCF's offices last spring were practically astronomical. Still, it wouldn't hurt to move the rancher's name to the top of the list.

"And where's home, Candy?"

"New York, of course." The brunette slid one slim leg across the other. "Me and Millie met at a casting call for an ad agency when Jimmy was just a baby. We was both trying to break into movies." She leaned forward, nodding the way people did when they had a secret to share. "It's tougher than anybody thinks. Anyways…" Candy thrust her shoulders back until the fabric of her T-shirt tightened. "I got the gig and Millie didn't, but we hit it off, you know? Millie, she didn't have much acting experience. And the kid only made it harder. I'd babysit when I could, but eventually Millie gave up and took a job waitressing. That's what got her killed. Some guy knifed her f' tip money."

Candy studied the floor. "After Millie died, it wasn't easy. I did my best by him, but it's been three months, and the kid still asks f' her. I took a job in Tampa over the holidays just so's I could bring him to you. I guess you'll take it from here." She shrugged and uncrossed her legs. "I got a life, too. You know?"

"Look." Sarah placed her hands flat on the desk. "The system doesn't work that way."

She scanned the notes she'd taken while Candy had

rambled on. Like acting, there was more to transferring a child into DCF's custody than one might think. And nothing, absolutely nothing, could be done before the first of the year when the computer system was up again.

"I'd need proof Jimmy is who you say he is. His birth certificate. Millie's death certificate. And that's just the beginning. We'll also need a home study to make sure you're able to provide a suitable environment for a little boy until his father can be located."

"Whoa, now." Candy's hands rose defensively. "I'm not keepin' him. I've done my part. As for those papers, I think I got everything you need right here." She reached into a voluminous bag and pulled out a raft of wrinkled forms.

Thumbing through them, Sarah had to admit they substantiated Candy's story. She smoothed the curled edges of a birth certificate listing Millicent Gage and Tyrone Parker as Jimmy's parents. An odd feeling stirred in the pit of her stomach as she traced the names with her finger, but she refused to jump to conclusions. Just because she knew one Ty Parker, that didn't make him this little boy's father. She'd worked for six months on his fraternity's ill-fated plan to sponsor foster kids on a cattle drive. He'd never once mentioned a wife… or a child.

She stared at the calendar that hung over Candy's head. She didn't need a computer to know the added pressure of the holidays had fractured some of the county's most at-risk families. As a result, every single bed in the foster care system had already been filled.

"You still can't leave him." Sarah slid the papers across the desk. "Until we locate his father, the only place I have available is a group home with a bunch of older boys." A bed in The Glades was definitely not the ideal situation for a young child. "It'd be better if Jimmy spent Christmas with you. And maybe New Year's. If you absolutely have to, you can bring him back then."

"Impossible." Candy rose, her arms crossed. "I've lined up a gig at The Pole Club in Tampa. Tips are very good this time of year, and it's not a place where I can take a kid, if you know what I mean."

A bitter taste rose in Sarah's throat. "What about Jimmy's father?" she asked. "What else can you tell me about him?"

A crafty sneer told her Candy recognized a stall when she heard one. The woman thrust a thumb toward the duffel bag still sitting on the floor outside the cubicle. "The kid's clothes are in there. And a picture of his mom. His dad? You'll have to track him down yourself. That's what you do, isn't it?"

Not really, thought Sarah. More of her work involved taking abused or neglected children *from* their parents than reuniting them. That part of her job was turning her into someone she didn't like very much. It was the reason her vacation was so important. Not just to take a break and recharge, but to make up her mind about where she went from here. Lately, she'd thought a lot about quitting. If it hadn't meant admitting defeat, she might have done it long ago. Her parents had never understood her career, and no wonder. Compared to her brother's groundbreaking work in physics or her sister's latest appearance at Carnegie Hall, her job at the DCF wasn't going to set the world on fire. But a decision about her future would have to wait until she found this latest abandoned kid a new home.

She tapped her pen against the desktop. A vague

description of "somewhere near Lake Okeechobee" wasn't going to help her locate Jimmy's father. Tracking him down meant legwork, hauling out the white pages and making thousands of calls. Unless…unless she hit the jackpot with her first spin of the wheel and the only Ty Parker she'd ever met was Jimmy's dad.

She gave the child's birth certificate another glance, but there was no time to dwell on Jimmy's parentage. Candy was on the move and, this time, there was no stopping her. Before Sarah could object, the woman blotted her lips on the boy's cheek and flounced out of the office.

Listening to the door swing shut, Sarah weighed her alternatives. There really was no choice. Not if she intended to spend a quiet Christmas packing for her Hawaiian vacation. A phone call to the housemother at The Glades was next on the agenda, and she turned toward her office, determined to make the call.

A tug at the hem of her shirt stopped her. She looked down into Jimmy's upturned face. The little boy was trying his best not to cry, but his eyes welled.

"What is it?" She steeled herself against an urge to kneel beside him and sweep him into her arms. The foster care system wasn't for the faint of heart, and even five-year-olds learned early to toughen up their act. The sooner Jimmy started, the better.

"Lady," he said, "did I miss Christmas?" He pointed to the box of ornaments and tangled tree lights Sarah had been packing. "Is it over?" His bottom lip trembled as he said the last word and tears spilled from his eyes.

It was too much. Sarah knelt and drew the child close.

"No, Jimmy, you didn't miss Christmas." His little-boy scent filled her senses. "Did you ask Santa for something special?"

Shopping for a present was the least she could do for a new orphan who'd spend the holiday with strangers. If they moved quickly, she could swing by one of the toy stores that stayed open for last-minute holiday shoppers and still have time to drop him off at The Glades.

"I…I…" Tear tracks ran down Jimmy's grimy cheeks. His mouth shook, but he stiffened, drawing courage from who knew where. "I need to see Santa. I hav'ta give him my Christmas list."

Sarah's thoughts raced. The odds of finding a shopping-mall Santa at this late hour weren't good. "I'm afraid he's busy loading his sleigh right now." She forced a bright smile. "If you tell me what's on your list, I'll make sure he knows."

"Can…can he…" Jimmy's shoulders slumped. He peered up at her, tears shimmering in his wide brown eyes. "Can Santa bring back my mom? I don't want any toys. I promise. I just want my mom."

"Oh! Poor baby." Only the worst sort of Scrooge could abandon this sad little boy on Christmas Eve. What did that make her?

Sarah hugged the child tighter. All too often, the system failed kids like Jimmy. The same way it was failing her. Not that she'd always wanted to become a social worker. Knowing the long hours and the tremendous workload, who would? But in her sophomore year at the University of Florida, a chance encounter with a friend from grade school had given new direction to her life. Meagan had experienced the worst of foster care. After learning her story, Sarah had switched her major from Education to Sociology so she could make a difference. So what had happened to Meagan wouldn't happen to any other kids.

But her idealistic plans to revamp the system had been buried under two years of working for a boss who valued computer upgrades over additional staff, of shifting children from one foster home to another, of seeing them falter and not being able to do anything to stop their downward spiral. It had practically wrung her dry. And lately, she'd started asking whether anyone was interested in fixing a system that didn't meet the needs of the children in its care.

But, if she could make a difference in one child's life—just one—didn't she have to do it?

She had to. That's all there was to it.

Lightly, she kissed the top of Jimmy's head while her dreams of a Hawaiian vacation faded.

TY PARKER SLID FROM Ranger's saddle, lifted his Stetson and ran his arm over his forehead. The long-sleeved shirt he'd put on fresh this morning clung like a second skin, now that he'd spent ten hours on horseback. He slapped his hat against his leg to dislodge the day's accumulation of dust. The move earned a derisive snort from the quarter horse.

"I hear ya, big guy," Ty said, grabbing the reins. "Let's get a drink and get outta this heat for a while." He aimed a glance at the sinking sun and wished someone would tell the weatherman not even Florida was supposed to be this hot the last week in December.

But hot it was. Hot and humid.

No matter. According to the almanac, they were due for another cold front. With any luck, it'd arrive about the same time as the wannabe cowboys who'd signed up for the Circle P's winter cattle drive.

In the barn, Ty grabbed a bottled water out of the fridge in the tack room. While Ranger drank his fill from a trough of clear-running springwater, Ty stopped to run his hand through hair that was two weeks overdue for a cut. Like every day on the thousand acres of palmetto and scrub that made up his South Florida ranch, there was more to do than twenty-four hours could hold. He shook his head, second-guessing his decision to hold a roundup so early in the season.

Not that it was any use. Done was done. Eight paying guests would arrive the day after tomorrow. Though he'd hoped for a bigger turnout, their fees more than covered the costs of an event that would serve as a warm-up for a larger, longer drive in the summer.

"And after last year, we could use the practice," Ty confided to Ranger as he went about feeding the black horse and settling him into his stall. That time, unforeseen complications had nearly proven disastrous. Thinking of the steps he'd taken to correct the situation, Ty grabbed the currycomb from its hook and set to work. He'd barely made a dent in brushing Ranger's dark coat when boots sounded on the barn floor.

"Hey, boss." Fifty-five years on the Circle P had etched furrows so deep around Seth's blue eyes that the man bore a permanent squint. He leaned against the lower half of the stall door. "Good ride?"

"It was pleasant enough." Ty ran the comb through sweat-matted hair on the horse's withers. "Spotted a couple of big rattlers down by Little Lake. We'll want to watch out for more of them next week, especially if it cools down a bit." The cold-blooded creatures frequently sought sunshine when the weather turned.

"I'll spread the word," Seth said, nodding. Rattlesnakes kept the rodent population in check, but a bite could be serious, if not deadly. "Cattle still hanging out near there?"

It was Ty's turn to nod. "Mostly around the salt lick on the north side. Should make roundin' 'em up easy enough."

"How many, you think?"

"The buyer wants fifty head," Ty answered as he worked his way down Ranger's side. The Andalusians he raised were known for their strong bloodlines and resistance to disease. "With the added help, it'll take two, maybe three days to get 'em in the pens." He smiled, knowing his ranch hands could do the job in an afternoon. Their paying guests might slow things down a bit, but the trade-off—money in the bank—was worth it.

"That ought to put us on the trail to Kissimmee by Monday."

Seth stole a piece of hay from Ranger's crib. "Sounds about right."

Though he practically had the schedule branded on his arm, Ty asked, "You still headin' to Fort Pierce tomorrow for supplies?" At the older man's affirmative grunt, he suggested adding sunblock to the list. "Cold weather or hot, a sunburn stings."

Seth leaned against the stall door and chewed as if he had all day and no place to go.

Ty shot him a look. In his thirty-two years he'd never known Seth to laze around. "You need somethin' else?"

"Well," Seth drawled, "that woman from DCF called again."

Ty's mouth slanted to the side. "Sarah Magarity? What's that make—four, five times?" She'd called on Christmas Eve and every day since. "She say what she wanted this time?"

"No. Just that she needs to talk to you on a—" Seth grinned, his voice hitting a high falsetto "—personal matter." He shifted his straw into the left side of his cheek. "I think she wants t' ask you out."

Laughter bubbled up from Ty's chest. The day the feisty caseworker thought of him that way, he'd share a pail of oats with Ranger. "Not much chance of that happening." He patted the horse's flank. "Not after the set-to we had the last time we saw each other."

"Oh?" Seth's sparse eyebrows knotted. "Hadn't heard about that. Guess she wasn't happy to hear those kids she sent us started a grass fire. What'd she say when you told her?"

"To tell the truth, the conversation never got that far." Ty ducked under Ranger's neck and began to work on his other side. The Big Brother program sponsored by his college fraternity had been his own personal way of honoring his best friend after J.D. died in Afghanistan. But the first batch of foster kids had been nothing but trouble with a capital *T.* He'd put up with the teens' shenanigans as long as he could. Still, some rules couldn't be broken. Starting a wildfire was one of them.

"She whisked those two juvenile delinquents into a conference room the minute my boots crossed the threshold. When she came out, it was clear they'd told some tall tales. She lit into me like a mama bear protecting her cubs." He'd had to admire the woman's spunk, even if she was wrong. "She blamed me, and made it clear in no uncertain terms that Alpha Rho wouldn't be sponsoring any more kids on my next roundup."

"You let her get away with that?"

"She didn't leave much choice, but it suited me just fine." He shrugged, recalling how the fiery redhead had marched him out of the DCF office, her cheeks so inflamed they matched her hair, the buttons of her sensibly tailored blouse straining with every breath. "I did manage to say those punks were born misfits, and there was nothin' in the world she could do to change it."

Seth chuckled. "Bet she didn't like hearin' that."

"Don't know. Don't care. I left before she could dish out any more of her nature-versus-nurture nonsense."

Or call Security, as the woman had threatened.

Ranger sidestepped, a move that telegraphed a growing unease.

Realizing he'd put a little more action into the brush than the job required, Ty slowed his strokes. "You sure she didn't say what she wants?"

"Yep, but based on what you just told me, maybe she finally realized how wrong she was and wants to apologize. Beats me why you'd have to go to her office, though."

"She wants me to come to her?" Ty clenched his teeth. The gall of women who thought they could crook their little finger and have men come running was beyond him. He'd had enough of that in the short time it had taken his marriage to fizzle. "Shoot." He shook his head. "I don't have time to drive into town."

"She seems pretty insistent." Seth sucked his teeth and spit. "Why don't you let me handle the chores here tomorrow, and you can go on the supply run. That way, maybe you can take Ms. Magarity out for a cup of coffee."

Ty aimed a sharp look at the ranch foreman. "You just want out of the trip, or you got something else in mind?" Lately, his nonexistent love life had been the subject of Seth's not-so-subtle hints.

"Well, it has been a while since you've been past the

Circle P's gate. And you're not gettin' any younger. Ya know you'll be tied up here till after the cattle drive."

Ty forced out a long breath. Ever since he'd quit his job as an investment broker and returned home, hanging on to the ranch that had been in his family for four generations had required every minute of his day. Six years ago, it had cost him his marriage. He hadn't gotten involved—not really—with another woman since then. Sure, there were days when he'd like to come home to something more than an empty house and an empty bed, but he'd have to be more than a little interested to drive as far as Fort Pierce for a date. And he wasn't interested in Sarah Magarity.

Why, then, six months later, did his anger over their argument still sting?

"You honestly think she wants to apologize?"

"What else could it be? Unless she's gonna ask you to take another couple of kids on the trail ride. Either way, she has to make nice."

Ty couldn't help thinking the two-hour drive might be worth the trip if it meant seeing a softer side of the argumentative woman who worked for the DCF. He bent low, examining Ranger's hooves one by one, certain Seth would offer a snide comment if the older man saw the look on his face.

"Fine," he said, straightening. "But there's a lot to be done if we're going to be ready when everyone gets here on Friday. You up for the job?"

"Have I ever let ya down?"

Ty stepped into the wide corridor between the stalls and hung the currycomb back on its hook. He trusted Seth, the same way his dad had relied on the man.

"Let's head on up to the house and compare notes,

then." He lifted a brow, teasing. "You think Doris'll have supper ready?"

"Beats me." Seth grinned. His wife, Doris, was the Circle P's head cook. She set supper on the table at six on the dot every night.

By the time he climbed into one of the Circle P's pickups at eight the next morning, Ty was certain Seth would have everything squared away in time for their guests' arrival. Having already put in a half day's work himself, he was surprised to find that he actually looked forward to relaxing a bit on the hundred miles of sparsely traveled, two-lane blacktop that stretched between the ranch and the nearest city. Not that he intended to waste the time. While he drove, he worked on the lyrics of a ballad he was trying to learn. Once he came within cell tower range, he turned off the CD player and concentrated on the ranch business he could handle by phone. No one answered at Sarah's direct line so he left a message saying he was on his way. The numbers on the dashboard told him it was a little after one when he finished his errands, including the much-needed haircut.

Inside the drab concrete-block building of the Department of Children and Family Services, Ty made his way between movable partitions that divided a large room into cubicles the size of Ranger's stall. Reaching an open area, he nodded to a little boy who looked up from the building he was creating out of small, red bricks. The child scrambled to his feet.

"Are you a real cowboy?" the boy asked, his mouth hanging open.

Ty glanced around to see if the boy's mother was close by, but there was no one within hailing distance. If Millie had stuck around, they'd probably have a passel of their own by now. But it hadn't worked out and he didn't know much about kids. This one was still staring so Ty twirled his best Stetson on one finger.

"You got me, kiddo. You like the boots?" He kicked out a foot.

"Uh-huh," the boy said. His head swung toward the end of the corridor. "Where's your horse?"

Ty let his voice deepen into a John Wayne-like gravel. "Back at the ranch."

"Oh." The little boy's shoulders slumped and with a wistful look down the hall, he turned and went back to his toys.

Ty ran a hand through his freshly washed hair and watched the kid's retreating back. Beyond the plain white walls, clear skies and balmy breezes had combined to make a perfect day on Florida's east coast. Why, then, wasn't the boy outside learning to ride a two-wheeler instead of cooped up in this office breathing stale recycled air? He shrugged, and with a final wave at the kid, moved farther down the hall.

Sarah Magarity's name hung outside a workspace slightly larger than the rest. Flowers perfumed her empty office, and he bent over pink blossoms whose fragrance reminded him of tropical islands and swaying palm fronds. He inhaled, appreciating the change from the odors of horse and cow, hay and sweat that usually filled his days. He glanced around, hoping to get a better sense of the woman who'd insisted on the meeting, but she didn't keep photographs on her desk. Rolling his hat brim through his hands, he settled onto a vacant chair and tried without success to block out the incessant ringing of telephones.

At last, he glanced into the corridor in time to catch sight of a slender foot wearing an open-toed shoe. The footwear was completely impractical, but it was pretty, and as its owner appeared in the doorway, his gaze rose past elegant ankles and trim calves to a loose-fitting business suit that effectively camouflaged womanly curves. He stood, extending a hand as he let his gaze wander Sarah Magarity's face. The hazel eyes that met his filled with unexpected emotion when her warm hand pressed into his grasp.

She swallowed visibly. "Mr. Parker, I know we didn't part under the best of circumstances last time, but I appreciate your coming in today. Please, take a seat."

"Most folks call me Ty." He remained on his feet until she was settled behind her desk.

"And I'm Sarah." She smiled one of those vague smiles people give when their thoughts are somewhere else.

Still wondering why she had demanded his presence, Ty waited while she opened a blue-edged folder and flipped through several official-looking documents.

"Mr. Parker—Ty," she said, looking up from the papers. "You were married to Millicent Gage, weren't you?"

"Millie?" Ty frowned. As far as expected topics of conversation went, his ex-wife was pretty far down on the list. He hadn't seen the woman in nearly six years, hadn't given her more than an occasional thought in the past two or three. He met Sarah's eyes. The concern he read there made him uneasy enough that he shifted in his chair.

"Ty," she said softly. "I'm afraid I have some sad news."

Sarah paused long enough for his mind to form a hundred different questions. Across from him, she drew in a breath so deep it made her chest swell.

"I'm very sorry to have to tell you that your ex-wife, Millicent, passed away a few months ago."

Millie. Dead?

Ty shook his head, trying to wrap his thoughts around the idea that the woman who'd been his childhood sweetheart was gone.

"How? Where?" he managed to ask.

"In New York. Apparently, she was mugged."

Nodding to himself, Ty absorbed this piece of news. Millie's hunger for more than a quiet life on the Circle P had driven them apart. He'd always hoped that she'd found someone else. Someone who would give her a brick house in the city, like the one she'd wanted him to buy. He brushed his hand over his face. Moisture had gathered in his eyes. He wiped it away and sighed.

Rising, he began, "Ms. Magarity..."

"Sarah, please," she interrupted.

He tried again. "Sarah. If that's why you called me here, you could have delivered that news over the phone and saved both of us some trouble."

"No, I couldn't."

"Why not? Millie walked out of my life a long time ago. I'm sorry she passed on, but it doesn't make sense that I'd have to come here so you could tell me about it."

He shook his head, cursing his foolishness for even considering that Sarah Magarity might be interested in him. Whatever he'd been thinking about her, he'd been wrong. The woman was so argumentative, she couldn't even deliver the news about his ex-wife without disagreeing with him.

Behind her desk, Sarah stood. Her soft features

hardened. “Aren’t you even going to ask about your son?” she demanded harshly.

“My… *What?*” Ty’s knees bent. His backside hit the chair again, this time hard enough to hurt.

Chapter Two

Beneath sun-darkened skin, Ty Parker went as pale as the glass of milk Sarah had poured for Jimmy that morning. The rancher sank onto the visitor's chair, his head bowed. A clean, manly scent filled the room when he ran his fingers through hair that fell like shocks of wheat across his forehead.

His reaction was so different from what Sarah had expected that she nearly forgot she'd been angry with him since last summer. One look at the child playing in the common area and her concern for Jimmy came back in a rush. She pushed aside her own feelings.

"Mr. Parker?" When he didn't budge, she put a little more intensity into her voice. "Ty, what are you going to do about your *son?*"

The man finally raised his head. The pain clouding his dark eyes stirred an urge to place a comforting hand on his shoulder. Grateful for the desk between them, she pressed her fingers against her thigh.

"I don't have a son," he said. "I don't have any children."

Sarah chewed her bottom lip. If she had a dollar for every time a father sat in her office and refused to take responsibility for his children, she'd be a rich woman instead of one who lived on a meager DCF salary. Besides, what earthly reason would Jimmy's mom have for keeping such a huge secret?

"It doesn't do any good to deny it." She let her back stiffen. "Now that Millie's gone, it's time you stepped up and became more than an absentee father."

"No." Ty shook his head. "You don't understand. Millie and I—" he stopped to mop his face "—our marriage fell apart long before she left. He's not mine. He can't be."

Everything about Ty shouted that this was the first he'd heard of his son. As much as Sarah wanted to give him the benefit of the doubt, the lengths some men took to get out of supporting their own kids never ceased to amaze her. She brushed aside Ty's objections with a wave of one hand.

"Doesn't matter. The fact is, your name—Tyrone Parker—is on Jimmy's birth certificate. In my book, that means you're responsible for him."

There wasn't a doubt in the world the rancher was Jimmy's dad. If she placed the photo she'd taken of the child under her hastily cobbled together Christmas tree next to one of Ty at five years old, she'd bet his own mother wouldn't be able to tell them apart. From deep-set brown eyes to thick blond hair, the two were as alike as father and son could be. She noted the wayward hairs that rose above Ty's careful part. He and the boy even sported the same cowlick. Sure, Jimmy was slight where Ty was muscular, but environment, not genetics, had made him that way.

"A piece of paper?" Ty came to his feet. "You think just because my name is on a birth certificate, that makes me this kid's father? I'm a cattleman. When we inseminate our cows, we demand DNA tests to confirm the sire. And that's what it'll take to prove this kid is mine."

Sarah pulled herself erect, squared her shoulders and did her best to ignore the way the tall man towered over her. Ty wasn't the first to deny he had fathered a child. He certainly wouldn't be the last.

"I've heard that before. More times than I can count. You want a paternity test? Fine. The way our labs are backed up with cases just like yours, it might take two weeks to get the results. In the meantime, there's a little boy waiting in the playroom. What am I supposed to do with Jimmy?"

Yes, even though it was against policy for a caseworker to get personally involved, she'd taken the child home on Christmas Eve. He'd been with her ever since. She'd told herself it was only a temporary measure, that without access to DCF's database, a kid could get lost in the system. It had happened before…in this very office…and she didn't like to think of the consequences. So, she'd broken a rule. Or two. This morning, she'd been called on the carpet for her actions. She might have jeopardized her next promotion, but the poor kid had no one else to love him.

What else was she supposed to do?

That didn't explain why she'd dipped into her vacation fund to give the boy a Christmas that fulfilled his every wish…except for the thing he wanted most, the one thing no one could deliver. She faltered. No good could come from letting the big rancher know how attached she'd grown to the child. His child.

"My supervisor wants the boy placed…today. If you insist he's not yours, I don't have any choice. I'll have to put him into The Glades."

Ty spared her a flinty look. "Those two idiots you

sent on my cattle drive last summer. They were from The Glades, weren't they? I thought that was only for teens. How many other little kids are housed there?"

Surprised Ty had bothered to learn a single fact about the two boys who hadn't lasted a week on the Circle P, Sarah wavered.

"It's not the ideal situation for a child as young as Jimmy," she admitted. Most of the residents at The Glades were old enough to be in high school and would age out of the system on their eighteenth birthdays. "We'll move him into a better placement—a foster home—as soon as a bed becomes available."

"And how long do you think that'll take?"

"Holidays can be terribly difficult for families. There's no way of telling when a spot will open up. It could be days. Weeks, even."

Ty expelled an enormous breath of air. "Let's get this straight. I don't believe for a second that this kid is mine. That long ago, I was struggling to hold on to the Circle P. Times were tough and my marriage was falling apart. But Millie would have told me if she was pregnant. Would have at least asked for money. And I'd have found a way to help her. No matter what. So, I'm telling you, this kid isn't mine. But..." He rolled his hat through his hands. His shoulders slumped. "But, I didn't exactly keep a calendar, if you know what I mean. On the off chance that the blood tests do come back positive, no kid of mine is going to spend one night in a place like The Glades. Have I made myself clear?"

Sarah patted a wisp of loose hair into place. By keeping Jimmy with her this past week, she'd not only forfeited her vacation, she'd gone out on a very thin limb. She'd be risking her job if she kept the child until the results came in. And there simply wasn't anywhere else for him to go. Not with Connie, her boss, in an uproar that Sarah had chosen the welfare of a child over the rules…again.

"It's the only option," she insisted.

"Well, he could come to the Circle P. At least until we get this mess straightened out."

Sarah let her eyes narrow. The look on Ty's face made it quite obvious he wasn't happy with the idea. "This isn't like one of your calves. You can't stick him in a stall and ignore him all day."

"We treat our cows better than that."

"So, you're saying you'll take care of him? Or you have someone who can?" Carefully, she considered the idea. As a prerequisite for the Big Brother program, Ty had sailed through the training course for foster parents.

The chiseled edge of his jaw firmed. "We have a roundup starting tomorrow, New Year's Day. He can come along." He glanced through the open doorway toward Jimmy. The way Ty nodded, Sarah thought the rancher might be talking more to himself than to her. "He can sit in the cook wagon with Doris, my foreman's wife. At night, he can bunk in with me and the ranch hands."

Sarah's breath caught in her throat. "You can't take a little boy on a cattle drive. It's too dangerous."

"Oh, it's not a real roundup. It's more of a camping trip." Ty paused. "On horseback." Another pause. "With cows." A grin worked its way across his mouth.

The smile ignited the same slow burn that had warmed Sarah's midsection back when she thought Ty and his pals from college might be able to give a couple of her older charges a fresh start. She caught herself staring at Ty's lips and bit her own. For Jimmy's sake, she had to ignore the man's mesmerizing good looks because taking a five-year-old on a trek into the wilderness just didn't make sense.

"Trust me. My family's been doing this for four generations. I wasn't much older than Jimmy when I went on my first one. The sunshine and fresh air will do the boy good."

"No. No. No." Sarah was already shaking her head. "I know all about your cattle drives, remember? Chris and Tom told me everything."

"Those two boys were hooligans who put other people in danger."

"That's not the story I heard."

She'd spent six months helping his fraternity sponsor two foster kids on the Circle P's annual cattle drive. The paperwork alone had been monumental, to say nothing of the hours she'd spent in meetings with Ty and his friends. In theory, a couple of weeks on horseback would help two of her most troubled charges turn their lives around. A plan that ended when Ty had practically hog-tied the boys and dragged them back into town after only two days.

"I heard all about the bottles that were passed around the campfire every night. You stuck two kids who'd never ridden before on horses and expected them to know what to do. They got lost and no one came to find them. There wasn't enough food—"

Ty's deep chuckles filled the space between them. "Doris would flat have a fit if she heard that."

Sarah's heart stuttered. Heaven help her, the man's smile seemed to out-shine the sun. She wrenched her gaze from his face and forced herself to stare at a spot over his shoulder.

"Look," he continued. "We all had high hopes for Alpha Rho's involvement with foster kids. No one's any sorrier than I am that it didn't work out. I know we had some problems, but none of that matters. What does matter is that I run a clean camp. Yes, my guests are free to bring their own liquor, but we see that everyone's well supervised. It's a family affair. Good, clean fun. We even have a couple of folks from Minnesota on this next ride. They're bringing their teenage daughter along."

Had the boys lied?

Sarah mulled the likelihood that she'd misjudged the rancher. Okay, the teens had been a bit on the wild side, but wasn't that the whole point? To expose them to a different environment in the hope that they'd make better choices in their lives?

That still didn't mean taking a five-year-old on a cattle drive was a good idea. Things would be different if Ty admitted he was Jimmy's father. The man's insistence that he wasn't changed the landscape. DCF rules would never permit a foster dad to take a child on a long trek through the wilderness, and she'd be fired if she approved it. But until the blood tests came back proving Millie had told the truth and Ty was wrong, she had no choice. She had to give this reluctant father a chance to get to know his son.

"All right, you can take him on your roundup with one condition." She paused long enough to give Ty a meaningful look that made it clear the stipulation was not up for negotiation. "I'm coming with him."

Surprise flickered across Ty's face. Amusement glinted in the eyes that slowly traveled over her. "Do you even know how to ride a horse?"

His frank appraisal made her nervous, and Sarah

crossed her arms. "Yes." She pushed her shoulders back, her chest out. "I'll have you know I rode dressage in college." Her part-time job at the Equestrian Center had meant more time mucking stalls than exercising the stock, but that was something Ty didn't need to know.

"Okay, then. I'll have my foreman, Seth, email you a list of supplies you'll need to bring." With another glance into the common area, his voice dropped. "Don't worry about the kid. I'll take care of whatever he needs. Just make sure you're both at the Circle P by noon tomorrow. We'll mount up and be on the trail by one. Now let's go see about that blood test." And without another word Ty Parker slipped his cowboy hat on his head and strode out of her office.

Sarah stared after him for a moment, wondering what she'd gotten herself into. The rancher, with his sun-bleached hair, piercing eyes and ruggedly handsome face, was easily the most attractive man she'd seen in ages. But looks weren't everything. Ty Parker opposed the goals she'd spent the past seven years trying to accomplish. So, why had she just volunteered to spend so much time in his company?

The answer to that was simple enough—for his son. The boy Ty refused to admit was his. The one who tugged on her heartstrings more than a seasoned DCF caseworker should ever allow. The child who was going home with her again tonight despite the hot water it would put her in.

Her eyes on Jimmy, Sarah picked up the phone and dialed the number for the lab.

THE FAINTEST SCENT OF TROPICAL flowers drifted in Sarah's wake as Ty held the door open for her and Jimmy. The woman smelled good—no denying it—but she was obviously in a snit over the way things had gone in her office. She practically marched along, a frown thinning her mouth to a tight line, her loose skirt swishing over her hips, Jimmy's hand securely in hers. The boy, who'd barely shed a tear when the nurse had jabbed an oversize needle into his arm, hurried to keep pace. Spying the purple gauze on the boy's thin arm, the same kind that wrapped around his own elbow, Ty winced.

The movement landed another blow behind his temples where a headache had hammered ever since the nurse asked Jimmy his birth date. It hadn't required a degree in math for Ty to count backward and realize Millie had indeed been halfway through her first trimester when she lit out for New York. He rubbed his forehead. For the life of him, he'd swear she'd quit sharing his bed months earlier, but maybe—just maybe—he was wrong. Time, and the miracle of modern science, would tell. Until then, the least he could do was watch out for the boy.

He caught up with Sarah and Jimmy outside the clinic where he gave the kid's shoulder a gentle squeeze.

"Thanks for holding my hand in there, pardner."

The little boy's hand slipped from Sarah's. His feet firmly planted on the sidewalk, Jimmy stared up at him through eyes clouded with doubt.

"You're not a real cowboy. You don't have a horse, and you were scared."

Even though the kid probably wasn't his, the accusation stung. Ty countered it by tugging on the brim of his Stetson. "I'm not, huh? You come on out to my ranch. You'll see."

"You have horses?" Excitement flashed across the boy's face. It faded quickly, though he was clearly awed by the prospect. Jimmy scuffed one sneaker against the ground and turned to Sarah. His voice dropped to a whisper. "I can't go there…can I?"

The little boy's attitude sent a chill down Ty's spine, and he winced. He couldn't fathom what life in New York had been like for Millie and Jimmy, but his ex-wife must have said "No, we can't afford it" more often than not if the child automatically thought something was out of reach. He bit back an urge to reassure the tyke. It wasn't his place. That honor belonged to Sarah.

"I guess you'd like that?" she asked the boy.

"Would I! There'll be horses. And cows. And… and…and…"

The joy fell out of Jimmy's eyes. A worried look took its place as his gaze shifted between the two adults. His lower lip trembling, he settled on Sarah. "Yeah, but, you'll come, too. Won't you?"

"I wouldn't miss it," Sarah said with far more enthusiasm than she'd shown all day.

Jimmy's eyes grew so wide Ty feared they might pop out of his head if someone gave the kid a good rap between his shoulder blades.

The boy's excitement was infectious. It tempted Ty to hang around for a while, and he considered asking the pair if they wanted to go for ice cream. But one look at Sarah stopped him. The smile she beamed into the child's excited face transformed her otherwise attractive features into downright heart-stopping. When Ty's pulse skipped a beat or two, he fought the urge to step closer with a reminder that he wasn't high on the prim and proper social worker's list of favorite people.

Watching them climb into a government-issue sedan a few minutes later, Ty tugged off his hat and mopped his forehead with one arm. Despite temperatures in the seventies, the cotton sleeve came away damp. And no wonder. It wasn't every day a man learned he might have a son. No matter how far-fetched the idea, he couldn't deny the thrill of possibility that had hummed through him ever since he'd heard the news.

A son!

A son to take fishing and play catch with in the backyard. A son to inherit the ranch he'd worked so hard to preserve. A son to carry the hopes, dreams and traditions of the Parker family into another generation.

But one who was rapidly approaching his sixth year on this planet without Ty hearing so much as a "Surprise! You're a dad" from his ex-wife.

Impossible.

With that sobering thought, he threw his hat into the pickup truck and slid onto the seat.

His marriage had hit the rocks not long after he and Millie had said their "I do's." Hindsight had eased the pain enough that he acknowledged his share of the blame. After high school, he hadn't been able to put enough distance between him and the ranch where he'd been born and raised. In college, he'd been sure he'd always feel that way. And Millie had counted on it. They'd planned a life in the city where Ty had promised to buy his wife the house she'd always wanted. But neither of them had factored in his dad's cancer. Ty had moved them home to help out, swearing it was just until his dad beat the disease.

Except, that never happened.

By the time they figured out it wasn't going to, the smell of hay and horses had become as much a part of Ty as red ink and sweet iced tea. He'd discovered a new love for the summer roundup, that he had a knack for raising cattle. Maybe it was in his blood. Devotion to their particular stretch of palmetto and scrub had flowed through Parker veins for nearly a century.

It hadn't flowed through Millie's, though, and she'd split.

What about Jimmy? Whose genes did he carry?

There was no denying the kid favored him, but no one had to tell Ty that looks could be deceiving. The Circle P's hardy breed of cattle traced back to the conquistadors. On the next ranch over, Ol' Man Tompkins raised Brahmas. Only Brahmas. Cattle with wide gray sides, a hump over their shoulders and a smell Ty couldn't abide. Two springs ago, Tompkins's heifers had started dropping brown-hided calves that looked a lot like Ty's cattle. His neighbor had about had a conniption, insisting one of Ty's bulls had found his way past the fence line. Blood tests had proven Tompkins wrong. The color was a throwback, but the calves were all Brahman.

So, as much as Ty hated to submit a little kid like Jimmy to a needle, testing his DNA was the only way to know for sure. He peeled off the strip of colorful gauze, stuffed it in the ashtray and grabbed his cell phone. Punching numbers, he reached out to the college roommate who'd stood at his side when he'd married Millie and gotten him drunk the night his divorce became final.

"Dave." Ty leaned against the seat back, picturing his friend behind an immense desk in a law office that overlooked Tampa Bay. "I've got a little problem." He waited a beat. "Millie's dead."

A sharp intake of breath preceded "Jeez, I'm sorry to hear that. You okay?"

"Yeah," he said past an odd tightness in his throat. "We hadn't seen each other, or even spoken, in years.

But that's not the problem. She had a baby. A boy. The birth certificate names me as the father."

"You're joking, right?"

"I wish I was," Ty said, not entirely sure he meant the words. "I'm in Fort Pierce where some friend of hers dropped the kid off at the DCF office like a sack of feed."

"Wait a minute." Through the receiver, Ty heard a chair squeak and knew Dave was staring at the ceiling, performing the same calculations that had been running through his own head. "Millie left—what? Six years ago? So the kid would be…"

"Jimmy—James Tyrone Parker—he's five. The dates mesh up. That doesn't make him mine. She would have said…something."

"Is there any possibility?"

"Not much of one. I've been racking my brain for all the good it's done me. Can't remember a single, well—you know. It was a bad time. I don't have to tell you how bad."

Ty's best friend had just been deployed to a war zone. Millie had seemed bent on turning their lives into one. And his dad had been dying. After he'd passed, it was Dave who'd safeguarded the Circle P, making sure ownership transferred to Ty rather than the army of creditors who'd demanded he sell the ranch. For that, he owed his friend far more than keeping Dave's freezer stocked with steaks.

A low whistle. "Whether he's yours or not, it sucks to be you."

"Tell me something I don't know." Either way, Millie had pulled off one heck of a cruel joke.

"How can I help?"

Ty ran a hand through his hair. "We just took the paternity test. Won't get the results for a couple of weeks. The question is, what do I do if I'm right and he's not mine?"

Another squeak of Dave's chair grated on Ty's nerves so much he wished he could pass his friend a can of oil.

"Yeah, that's the bad part. According to Florida law, if you and Millie were still married when the kid was born—"

"We were. The divorce didn't become final for another couple of months."

"Then, he's yours. No matter what the blood tests say."

Ty nodded and swallowed hard. He was either a stranger to the son he'd never known about or dangerously close to getting stuck with some other man's child. Both options made him sick to his stomach. "And there's nothing I can do?"

"As a probate lawyer, that's not exactly my field of expertise. I think you can go to court, give up your rights, but I'll have to look into it. Fax whatever paperwork you have to my office. I'll have something for you in a couple of days. And, Ty?"

"Yeah?"

"Sorry to hear about Millie."

"Me, too, man," he said, thinking of the mess his ex-wife had left him to clean up. "Me, too."

Ending the call, he threw the truck in gear and headed for the closest shopping mall. A glance at the dashboard clock told him it'd be dark by the time he unloaded the supplies and the few items he'd pick up for Jimmy. Later still, by the time he'd sit with Doris and Seth, let them in on the secret he and Sarah had decided to keep from the boy until the test results came back. Before he turned in, he'd hunt down the old trunk that held the boots he'd worn as a kid. Jimmy was a might on the small side, but Ty bet there'd be a pair or two that would fit the boy.

He smiled, remembering the way the child's face had lit up at the idea of spending time on the ranch. His son or not, he'd do whatever it took to make sure the kid enjoyed the next ten days on the trail. And who knew, he might even convince Sarah he wasn't the ogre her foster kids had made him out to be. Changing the uptight social worker's opinion would be a challenge, no doubt about it. But life was a challenge and, as he made the final turn onto the road that would take him home to the Circle P, Ty determined to meet this one head-on.

"WHAT'S THAT KID DOING HERE? I thought we agreed earlier that you'd take him to The Glades."

Busted.

Sarah gripped Jimmy's case file so tightly the thin manila practically folded in two. She'd hoped that with their tracking system off-line, Connie would forget about the boy. She should have known better. Just like she should have guessed that her supervisor would report to work though their office was officially closed. Connie wouldn't let a little thing like having no computers stop her. She'd just work longer, harder.

Until she keeled over at her desk or reached the age of mandatory retirement.

Studying her boss's wiry gray hair and hardened features, Sarah wondered if she was looking at herself in twenty years. She'd transferred to Fort Pierce in order to learn from the best the DCF had to offer, but all she'd learned so far was that the foster care system was broken and she'd never be able to fix it. Not by working from within. Every time she tried—the way she had with Jimmy—she put her career on the line.

"I've located his dad," Sarah offered from the doorway to her manager's office.

At least, she'd spoken with the man listed on the child's birth certificate and knew someone wasn't telling the truth. Either Millie had falsely named Ty or she hadn't told him about his son. And after staring into a pair of eyes the same earthy-brown as Jimmy's, Sarah would put her money on the latter. "I thought you'd want the child placed with his father."

"So, why is he here? Shouldn't he be with his dad?"

"According to Ty—" The name felt too familiar on her tongue, and Sarah backtracked. "According to Mr. Parker, until yesterday he never even knew he had a son. He's asked for a day to prepare." She took a deep breath. "Plus, I'm not entirely sure about him."

Behind the rimless glasses perched on her nose, Connie's stern look deepened. "You have doubts about this man? Why is that?"

"It's—" Sarah fought back a sigh "—complicated."

How much of the truth could she tell the DCF supervisor? Certainly not that seeing Ty stirred her blood in ways she hadn't experienced in far too long. Or that his good looks made her doubt her own judgment. She could barely admit those things to herself, much less say them out loud.

Nor could she confide that Ty had demanded a paternity test. Constance Morgan didn't just run the DCF by the book, she'd written it. Literally documented the code social workers followed in order to protect children throughout the state. If she learned the rancher had challenged Jimmy's paternity, she'd lock the little boy in the system until the test results came back. And if there was one thing—maybe the only thing—Sarah agreed with Ty about, it was that neither of them wanted Jimmy placed in a group home.

"We've dealt with him before. He's the rancher who runs that old-fashioned cattle drive from Okeechobee to Kissimmee each summer."

Connie nodded. "I remember. His fraternity wanted to start a Big Brother program. You spent months working on the project, even though I told you it would fail. These do-good programs usually do." She propped her elbows on the edge of her desk, her fingers tented, her chin resting on her thumbs. "I can see why you'd question his abilities to parent. But we'll monitor the situation. Do what we can to see him through this initial transition. Intervene, only if we have to."

"Well, that's the problem." Sarah shook her head. "His midwinter roundup starts tomorrow. It lasts about ten days. He plans to take the boy with him."

"Ten days?" Connie's eyebrows knitted and her lips turned down at the corners. "No hope of salvaging your trip to Hawaii?"

"I tried," Sarah said with a grimace she didn't have to fake. She'd checked with her travel agent. The islands' tourist season was in high gear, the out-of-the-way locations where flowers for her tropical garden were at their best, solidly booked through spring. And there was the little matter of the woman she'd hired to look after her tropical plants. According to their contract, she'd have to pay for the service no matter what.

Sarah sighed. Her plumeria and orchids liked humidity and needed plenty of water. The way she babied them, sometimes, she thought she'd be better off with cats. "It'll be months before I can reschedule."

"And you want to accompany the boy." A statement, not a question.

Sarah fought the urge to duck her head when Connie's glasses slid down her nose. The older woman's steely-eyed focus bore down on her.

"If you do this, you'll have to do it on your own time."

"I figured as much." Technically, she already was on vacation. If she didn't go on the cattle drive, she'd only spend the entire time worrying about Jimmy when, instead, she could be right there beside him.

"And you're up for this?"

This was it, her one and only chance to back out.

"It'll be a stretch," she admitted, letting her gaze drift toward Jimmy. As if he sensed her, the boy looked up from the video game he'd found under the tree Christmas morning. He waved, and Sarah wiggled her fingers in return. She couldn't ignore the way the child's lopsided grin tugged at her heart. Nor would she risk his safety by sending him off into Florida's back country with a man she didn't completely trust.

Even if he was the boy's father.

Even if one look at the tall, muscular rancher made all her nerve endings stand at attention.

She'd keep *those* feelings under control. For Jimmy's sake—and her own—she'd maintain an objective, professional demeanor. After all, it wasn't as if she and Ty would be riding off into the sunset together. They were going on a cattle drive. Where the dirt and the dust, the sweat and the smell of cow droppings weren't exactly romantic. As long as she kept her guard up, she could ignore the not-so-tiny flare of attraction she felt for Ty Parker and concentrate on the more important issue—giving Jimmy the future he deserved.

A single glance at the boy told her it was worth the risk. But in order to help the child, she'd have to stay objective. Which, with Ty in the immediate vicinity, might pose a bigger task than she could handle.

Chapter Three

"'Bout ready to hit the trail, boss?"

Ty quirked an eyebrow at Matt Henson's fake drawl. The accountant from Chicago would never make it as a Southerner. Not with an accent that was more cream of wheat than grits. But the man, who readily admitted he'd lived his entire life above the Mason-Dixon Line, had apparently fallen in love with the image of himself as a rough and ready cowboy on last year's roundup. He loved it so much, in fact, that he and his brother had convinced three of their friends to join them for the winter cattle drive.

"Pretty soon."

Ty grinned. He couldn't fault Matt or the others for wanting to mount up and ride. To tell the truth, he was a might eager to hit the trail, himself. There was nothing quite as good as a long day in the saddle to help a man forget his troubles. Troubles, Ty had in spades. Between his struggle to keep the ranch in the black and Sarah Magarity's surprising news, worry pressed heavily on his shoulders.

He lifted his hat and brushed one hand through his hair. In the large, open yard, ranch hands darted here and there, loading supplies and suitcases into sturdy trucks outfitted to look like covered wagons. Ty knew without checking that Doris was in the kitchen, filling huge coolers with pies and cakes and the various side dishes she'd spent the past month preparing. Determined to give his customers the experience of a lifetime, one they'd paid well for, he refused to let the drive be waylaid by a few latecomers. He shaded his eyes to scour the long dirt drive. Nothing. A quick glance into the cloudless sky where the sun hung a hand's width west of straight overhead told him one o'clock was on fast approach with no sign of his last two guests. If Sarah and Jimmy didn't show soon, he'd have no choice. He'd have to leave without them.

Had the feisty redhead ignored his objections and stuck Jimmy in The Glades?

Maybe it was for the best. In all likelihood the kid wasn't his, and being around Sarah only complicated his life. Now, if he could only get that through to his subconscious, he might be able to get some rest. Last night, it seemed all he'd done was toss and turn. When he had finally fallen into a uneasy sleep, his dreams had been plagued by images of a redhead whose kissable mouth smiled only for him.

Ty slapped his hat against his leg and forced his thoughts back to the cattle drive. Nodding toward the corral that held a dozen horses, he led the way to the rail.

"Did you pick yourself a good one this year, Matt?"

Not that the would-be cowboy could pick a bad one. Ty noted the solid horseflesh milling about the crowded pen. He and Seth had considered every mount on the ranch before choosing the best from among their working stock. Each of the horses was used to herding cattle. Each had its own personality and, with enough spirit to set them above the average dude ranch nag, not one of them would blindly plod along nose-to-tail down a dusty road.

As he and his guests discussed the relative merits and drawbacks of the horses, Ty fought to keep from scratching his head in frustration. Usually, preparing for the cattle drive buoyed his spirits. But today, his thoughts kept wandering where he didn't want them to go. While he assigned the gentlest horses to the Garrison family—a father, mother and preteen from just outside St. Paul—he worried that Sarah had made a wrong turn. Helping Matt with a headstrong gelding, he shoved aside that idea. GPS devices practically guaranteed folks they'd reach their destination, and Sarah didn't strike him as the type to wander about aimlessly. By the time Matt's brother, Elliott, and their three friends chose their mounts, Ty couldn't ignore the facts.

Sarah and Jimmy were no-shows.

At that thought, the hollow spot below Ty's ribs began to ache. Should have eaten lunch, he told himself, refusing to believe the missing social worker had anything to do with it. Preparing to have everyone mount up and hit the trail, he shot a last look down the road. This time, a plume of dust rose from behind a small, serviceable sedan. Despite himself, Ty felt a bead of sweat trickle down his neck.

The car pulled to a halt across the yard in front of the ranch house, where the other guests had parked. Sarah emerged from the vehicle first. As she had the last time they'd met, she wore what Ty called her working uniform—a loose skirt and blousy jacket. He frowned at the clothes, wondering why she hadn't taken the time to change. His expression tightened when one of the businessmen—John Padgett, he thought—gave a low, appreciative whistle.

Ty shot the guy a look. "Keep it clean," he warned.

A lopsided grin was his reward. "Not to worry, boss," John answered as Sarah retrieved two tote bags and an armload of clothes from the trunk. "The kid's a deal breaker."

Ty swung back to the car where Jimmy had clambered out and stood holding Sarah's hand. The little tyke was practically jumping up and down, pointing to the horses in the corral, the covered wagons, the stacks of duffel and gear bags waiting to be loaded.

The kid's joy was so infectious Ty felt a grin tug at the corners of his mouth. Sternly, he ordered himself not to let his guard down, not to get too close. The boy wasn't his. He couldn't be. Just because Jimmy had blond hair and brown eyes like his own, it didn't mean they were related.

Hell, his best friend, J.D., had looked like him, too, but no one ever mistook them for brothers. At least, not after they were fully grown. Their height alone had set them apart. Ty hadn't stopped growing till he hit six foot three where J.D. had barely grazed the six-foot marker when he wore cowboy boots. Ty's throat tightened at the memory of his friend. He wrenched his thoughts away from the flag-draped footlocker stored in his attic.

Striding across the dusty yard, he couldn't trust his voice and tipped his hat to Sarah in tight-lipped silence. A quick ruffle of Jimmy's hair helped him get his bearings, and he bent low to ask, "Believe I'm a cowboy now, pardner?"

"Uh-huh," the boy answered, his grin spreading until Ty was sure it couldn't get any wider.

"I'd about decided you weren't going to make it." He turned to face the woman who'd shown up more than an hour late.

"Sorry. I had to deal with a crisis before I left the office. Then, getting the signed authorization for this trip took a little longer than I expected."

He aimed a pointed glance at the jeans and shirt draped across her thin arm. "You can head on up to the house. Bathroom's down the hall on the left."

From the frown that crossed Sarah's face, he knew she was weighing the pros and cons of taking the boy with her.

"He'll be okay with me for a bit." Honing in on the child, he said, "I was just heading into the barn to check out a new foal. That's a baby horse," he added for Jimmy's sake. "Help me with these bags and you can come with me while Ms. Sarah changes clothes."

He grabbed the closest duffel bag. The thing weighed forty pounds if it weighed an ounce, and he groaned. "What do you have in here, rocks?"

Sarah's shoulders straightened. Her voice dropped from guarded to prim disapproval. "Your list was quite extensive. Those items, plus my laptop, cell phone, the chargers—I can't help it if it's too heavy for you. You want me to carry it?"

Ty's sideways glance caught the dare flashing in Sarah's hazel eyes. He tore his gaze away from hers. The woman had a handle on bossy, but she obviously hadn't been paying attention when he explained the logistics back in her office. Generations of Parkers had ridden in the summer roundup. Over the years, sure, they'd added a few amenities. But the rustic bunkhouses dotting the trail provided little more than shelter from the sun and the rain.

When he'd developed a plan to open the cattle drive to tourists, he'd considered outfitting the cabins with electricity. Eventually, he'd decided against it. His bottom line had something to do with that choice, but more important, he wanted to preserve the old ways, give his guests a taste of Old Florida. Which meant cooking over an open fire, lighting their way with lanterns, turning in shortly after the sun set and rising early. No air-conditioning, televisions or laptops. He thought he'd made all that clear. From the way Sarah stood, hand on one hip, maybe he needed to explain it again. He dropped her bag in the dirt.

"Might as well leave all your electronics here. There's no place to charge them till we get to Kissimmee."

The challenge in Sarah's eyes shifted to concern.

"No electricity?" She nibbled her lower lip the way he'd seen her do in her office. Her eyes darted from the bag to the car and back. "The battery's good for eight hours. I brought a spare. If I'm careful and only check in with the home office once or twice a day, they should last."

Ty tilted his head to one side and let his eyes narrow. "Check in?"

"Yeah, email."

He suppressed a grin. "Unless someone planted a Wi-Fi connection in the middle of a palmetto bush, that's not gonna work."

Sara sighed. "Okay. I can call if I have to."

He ran a hand through his hair. She really didn't get it, did she. "By tonight, we'll be pretty far beyond range of the closest cell phone tower." He fought the urge to run his thumb along her lip as she bit down hard enough to turn the pink flesh white.

"Okay, then." The look on her face shifted to one of understanding, if not acceptance. "While I'm inside, I'll let the home office know I'll be out of touch for a while." She motioned to the heavy duffel bag. "I still have to bring my laptop. I need it to write reports."

About me, no doubt. Ty tossed Sarah's bag into the back of the luggage cart. He shrugged aside the tiniest flicker of anxiety. Sarah could write all the reports she wanted; they wouldn't change the fact that Jimmy wasn't his. He reached for his most disarming smile.

"Sure, go on up. Doris is probably in the kitchen. But first, if you don't mind, let's get everyone introduced proper-like so we can head out soon as you're ready."

He quickly went around, introducing Jimmy and Sarah to the five pals from Chicago, followed by Tom and Hope Garrison, their daughter Kelly. While the ranch hands helped everyone else saddle their horses, Ty held his hand out to Jimmy.

"Ready to see that pretty little colt and his mama now?" he asked. After getting an encouraging look from Sarah, the child slipped his small hand into Ty's larger one.

For a beat or two, Ty wondered what it'd be like if Jimmy depended on him all the time. He shook his head. It'd be one thing if his blood ran in the kid's veins, but it didn't. Sooner or later, everyone would figure that out. Then Sarah would find the boy's real father, a man who'd give the kid a home. Till then, he might have a moral obligation to make sure the child was taken care of, but getting close to a kid who'd never be his didn't make much sense.

That didn't keep him from grinning at the boy's efforts to match his stride as they crossed the bustling yard. Ty kept a watchful eye out, steering them well clear of dangerous hooves. He held tight to Jimmy's hand until they reached the nearly deserted barn. In its cool interior, he relinquished his grip and let the boy run on ahead. Drawn by soft nickers from a stall two doors down, the child rushed to the door and peered through the gaps between the wooden slats.

"Oh, cool," he whispered.

Ty leaned against the top of the Dutch door, his own smile widening. Used to human company, the mare barely paid them any attention. The colt was another matter. On impossibly thin legs, the young horse moseyed over to investigate the visitors. When he nosed the gap where Jimmy stood, the boy giggled.

"I think it likes me," he exclaimed.

"I'm sure he does," Ty nodded. The colt came from good stock. "The mom is called a mare. Her name is Ocita."

The name meant *powerful,* a good name for one whose bloodlines traced back to the first horses in the New World. Ty looked down at the kid, whose attention was solidly focused on the colt, and decided to skip the history lesson.

"The baby is Niceta. His name means *victorious.* He's only two days old." He pointed to the white streak that ran down the center of the colt's dark face. "Pretty, isn't he?"

"Yeah," Jimmy whispered. He stared through the slats in openmouthed admiration while Niceta blew air and snorted.

Backing up a step, the little boy laughed nervously.

"That's just his way of getting to know you," Ty explained. He reached down to scratch the colt's forelock. "He's a sweet thing and won't hurt you. Want to pet him?"

Jimmy stared at him, his eyes as round as half dollars. "Can I?"

"Sure." The boy's awe awakened memories of the first time Ty had ever seen a young horse. A warm spot opened in his chest. "Bet he'd like it if you rubbed his head. Here, let me hold you up so you can reach him." He hefted the child, surprised at how thin and light the kid felt in his arms.

Jimmy planted a few tentative pats on the young horse's head before he swiveled a look to see if Ty approved. But there wasn't a wrong way to get acquainted, and Ty thought it best to let the two youngsters figure it out on their own. Evidently, his method worked because Jimmy was quickly engrossed with the task while Niceta leaned so close to the door he was practically pushing against the slats in an effort to get nearer.

"I think you've made a friend there." The poke in the ribs he gave the kid earned a giggle. Ty swallowed and set the child on the ground. Guarding his heart against a boy who took such honest joy in the simple act of petting a horse was going to be tougher than he'd thought.

"Ty? Hey, Ty." The ranch foreman's voice echoed through the nearly empty stable.

"Yeah, Seth?" Ty leaned out into the aisle where he could be seen.

"I need ya to take a look at this cinch. Not sure, but I think we'll have to replace the saddle on Sad Sack." Seth stood in the center of the big barn door holding the reins of the horse Ty had assigned to Kelly Garrison.

"Be right there," Ty called. He looked down at the kid, who was still engrossed in petting the foal.

The little boy glanced up at him. "Can I stay here? Please?"

Ty swung a look at Seth who stood not fifty feet away. The kid wouldn't be out of his sight for more than a second or two. "No climbing on the stalls. And you won't wander off?"

Pale yellow hair bobbed up and down. "Sure, Mr. Ty. I just want to watch him a little more."

Ty tipped his hat back so he could look Jimmy straight in the face. "Okay, then. You stay right here and don't move. I won't be long."

Just to be sure, he quickly checked the surrounding area for dangerous tools. The stable was neat and orderly, just the way he liked it. Ocita and her colt were the only horses still in the barn and they were safely locked in their stall. As long as the kid did what he'd been told, he'd be fine.

"On my way, Seth," he called, feeling confident that he and the child had reached an understanding.

DISMISSED. TY PARKER had summarily dismissed her, turning his full attention to Jimmy. Sarah tried telling herself she was glad about that. Wasn't it exactly what she'd wanted, for the man to acknowledge his son and assume responsibility for him?

Angry at herself for nearly giving in to a jealous twinge—and at Ty for being, well, Ty—she tried stomping into the ranch house, a move that would have gone much smoother if she'd been wearing flats or boots instead of shoes with three-inch heels. Heels that sank into the dust and dirt, miring her so deep into the gray sand it was a miracle she made it to the steps upright and with her dignity intact.

Her emotional balance was another matter. She'd been slowly losing that since the day Ty and his fraternity brothers had walked into the DCF office to propose their Big Brother program. The man defined "easy on the eyes." His desire to help foster kids, along with boyish charm and a great smile, had pushed all of her buttons. But they'd never seen each other without two or three of his fraternity brothers in the room. After the experiment had failed, she'd been too angry with him to feel even the slightest spark of attraction. Now that they were on his ranch, where it was her job to help him learn to be a parent, she wasn't sure how long she could maintain the air of a stern social worker who did everything by the rules. The tall, handsome rancher's laugh stirred an odd sensation in her chest. She'd had to fight to keep from smiling at him.

Which wouldn't do. It wouldn't do at all.

Gaining the stairs, she stomped up the wooden planks. Her heels sounded a staccato beat across the wide-railed porch. The screened door gave a satisfyingly loud squeak when she tugged on the handle, and she stepped into the darkened interior of the house, letting the door slap shut behind her.

Safely out of Ty's sight, Sarah slowed, stopping long enough to regain her composure and get her bearings. Her frown deepened. When she'd pictured the bachelor's ranch house, an attractive great room hadn't been part of it. And especially not such a smartly designed tile entry that led to cedar floors burnished to a coppery-red. Their satiny finish silently urged her to slip out of her shoes and glide across the wood in stockinged feet. Her gaze crept over a cream-colored sofa positioned in front of a towering stone fireplace. A chocolate afghan at one end of the couch all but called out for someone to curl up beneath it with a favorite book…or a favorite rancher.

Sarah ran a hand through her hair, banishing the

image before it had a chance to take root. There'd be no hanky-panky with Ty Parker. The brush of his fingers might ignite nerve endings that had gone far too long without a man's touch. His very presence might tempt her to throw the rule book out the window. But she was there for a purpose, and one purpose only. To determine if the man who refused to admit he had a child could be a father to the boy who had stolen her heart.

Down the hall on the left stood a spacious guest bath where she quickly changed out of her workday clothes and into a snug pair of jeans and a tank top. Shoving her feet into a brand-new pair of boots, Sarah ignored the uncomfortable way they pinched her toes while she pushed aside the niggling feeling that she should rush back out to the yard. Much as her heart tugged in that direction, she was there to help Jimmy bond with his father, something that couldn't happen unless they spent time alone together.

She turned in the opposite direction. A long hall lined with framed pictures beckoned. She slowed in front of a shot of a cute youngster who, just as she'd suspected, looked exactly like Jimmy. A few steps farther, she lingered over a photo taken in front of the ranch house. The resemblance between Ty and the couple in the picture was so strong she was certain they were his parents. From the background information he'd supplied the DCF last year, she knew Ty had lost his mother in a car accident the summer before he started high school. Cancer had taken his dad a few years later.

There were other photographs—younger versions of the rancher with friends or cousins. One of Ty with a man in uniform. Sarah smiled at the silly grins both men wore as they mugged for the camera, their arms draped about each other's shoulders.

She scanned the hall, but there were no pictures of Millie. Would Ty dig some out once the paternity tests proved he was Jimmy's dad? The single, crumpled photo in the boy's backpack was the only picture he had of his mom. He deserved so much more. Determined to get it for him, Sarah squared her shoulders.

At the end of the hall, she gaped at a kitchen where stainless steel counters and sinks provided enough prep space for a small army of cooks. An enormous stove—the largest she'd ever seen—dominated the far end of the room and she blinked, wondering how one would brew a cup of tea on such a monstrosity. Wanting to help out, she aimed a friendly smile toward the plump, matronly looking woman who was busy taking dishes from one of two Sub-Zeros and stacking them into coolers.

"Hi," she called from the safety of the doorway. "You must be Doris. Ty—um—Mr. Parker, said you'd be here. I'm Sarah. Can I help you with anything?"

Two pies balanced in her age-spotted hands, Doris slowly straightened. The woman's eyes swept Sarah with a sharp, appraising look.

"Ty mentioned you. And that little boy. Millie's son."

"Ty's son," Sarah corrected. They'd agreed to keep the news from Jimmy until the test results came back, but she knew Ty had confided in Doris and her husband, Seth, the foreman.

The older woman flipped a long white braid over one shoulder. "That remains to be seen, doesn't it?"

"From all the pictures—" she gestured over her shoulder "—I'd say there wasn't much doubt. Jimmy looks just like Ty did when he was a boy."

"Huh." Doris's mouth twisted. "That Millie was a piece of work. Always pushin' Ty to move into town.

Take a real job. Like running the Circle P wasn't good enough for her. She never did make a lick of sense. But to run off without telling anyone she was pregnant…"

Sensing the opportunity to learn more about Jimmy's mother, Sarah edged close enough to lean against a counter. "So, six years ago, no one even guessed?"

"Has it been that long?" Doris lowered the two pecan pies into the waiting cooler before answering her own question with a nod. "That sounds about right. She split the same day we got the news about the Dalton boy, so I reckon it was." Her hands rested atop one of the steel tables. "That was a bad day," she whispered. "A very bad day."

"An accident?"

Doris shook herself. Her head tipped until she looked Sarah square in the face.

"Nah, J.D. was in the army. He hadn't been in Afghanistan but a few days when he lost his life to a roadside bomb."

"Oh, I'm so sorry." Sarah stopped, thinking about the young soldier in the photograph. "Is that his picture in the hallway?"

Another nod. "His family didn't come from nothin' so he mostly grew up here on the ranch, alongside Ty." A faint smile played on Doris's lips. "Them two was thick as thieves. More like brothers than friends. J.D., he even listed Ty as his next of kin." She shook her head, the sound of her deep sighs filling the kitchen. "The day that black sedan pulled up out front and those two uniformed officers stepped out, that was a rough one. By nightfall, Millie, she'd run off, too."

Sarah sucked in a breath. Ty had certainly suffered more than his share of loss in his thirty-two years. To lose his best friend and his wife on the same day, well…

no wonder the man felt bitter. She raised her head, suddenly aware that Doris had continued talking.

"By then, things had been bad between Ty and Millie for a while. Everybody knew it was just a matter of time before she split." Doris folded her arms across her chest. Her voice took on a defensive tone. "I don't care if she is dead, I'll never forgive that child for running off the way she did. She should have at least seen Ty through J.D.'s funeral."

Sarah closed her eyes, trying to imagine herself in Millie's situation. Pregnant and trapped in a marriage that wasn't working. The house in an uproar over the news about J.D. It seemed coldhearted, mean even, for Millie to choose that particular day to leave, but it certainly wasn't the oddest tale she'd heard in seven years with the DCF. As a social worker, all too often she saw the worst side of people. Mothers who hit their children. Husbands who abused their wives. Foster parents who exploited the system and the innocent lives entrusted to them.

"I guess we'll never know why she did what she did, but at least Millie kept the baby. She did her best to create a home for Jimmy. And now Ty has the chance to do the same thing. What do you think—is he good father material?"

Sarah fought the urge to squirm beneath Doris's laser-sharp stare.

"*If* Jimmy's his, Ty'll do right by his child." She closed the lid on the cooler, hefted it into her arms and headed for the door. Her parting shot drifted over one shoulder. "If not...my guess is he'll be your problem."

Sarah ground her back teeth. Though the thought of leaving the little five-year-old in The Glades made her sick to her stomach, the alternative wasn't much better. Even if Jimmy started out with good foster parents, the situation wouldn't last—it never did. By the time he aged out of the system at eighteen, he'd have spent time in half a dozen homes. Maybe more.

The kid deserved better. Every child did. They deserved to grow up in stable environments. In homes with people who loved them. She had tried without much success to make that happen for the kids under her care in the DCF. But she'd sworn to make a difference one life at a time. Right now, she had the opportunity to do that with Jimmy. If things didn't work out with Ty, she'd find somebody to love the little boy who'd lost his mother and might never find his father.

Somebody like her?

She flicked a stray crumb from the countertop. There was bending the rules, and then there was breaking them outright. Getting approval to keep Jimmy, raise him as her own, yeah, that would do more than break the rules. It would smash them to bits. And it was never going to happen. Not as long as she worked for the DCF.

She paused, a fresh understanding of just how broken the system was washing over her. She'd gone into social work vowing to make some changes. So far, the only thing changing was her...and she didn't like having to harden her heart because there were too many kids and too few good parents. Every time well-intentioned people like Ty and his fraternity brothers gushed about new plans but gave up when the first thing went wrong, she lost a little more faith.

She took a breath. There was no use fretting needlessly. The photos in the hallway had shown exactly what she'd expected—Jimmy was the spitting image of Ty as a child. The blood tests would prove he was Jimmy's father. Of that, she had no doubt.

Emerging from the ranch house minutes later, Sarah spied Ty's long, lean form striding swiftly across the crowded yard. The man moved with an easy grace, his loping gait sensuous and at the same time purposeful. Sarah swallowed and wrenched her gaze away, sweeping the busy yard where horses and people milled about before her focus circled back to Ty. This time, she studied the empty spot at his side. Her boots were in motion almost before her mind registered the child missing from the picture.

Trying to mask her fear, she waited until she reached the rancher before she demanded, "Where's Jimmy?"

Ty looked down at his feet as if he expected the child to materialize there.

"Where is he?" she repeated. "I left him with you for fifteen minutes. You were supposed to watch him."

"Relax. He's fine."

The easy drawl made it sound as if the man didn't have a care in the world, but he couldn't hide the flicker of unease in his eyes. Ty wasn't as certain as he sounded.

"Yeah, well, where is he?"

"He's in the barn. He wanted to spend more time with Ocita and her colt."

"You left him alone? With horses?" Sarah hated the way her voice shrilled, but seriously, the man was clueless. And she'd been just as dumb, trusting him to take care of a child. She brushed past him and raced for the barn, the sound of the rancher's heavier footsteps close on her heels.

Chapter Four

Ty stared at the patch of bare floor where he'd left Jimmy five, maybe ten, minutes earlier. A sinking feeling in his stomach descended so low his toes threatened to curl.

Where was the kid?

He hadn't intended to let the boy out of his sight, had kept one eye on the child while he replaced the saddle on Sad Sack. Then…then, one of the businessmen had asked for his help. And someone else after that.

His head pounded as he brushed past Sarah. Reaching Ocita's stall, Ty grabbed the rough wood of the first slat hard enough to feel splinters gouge his palms. He threw a look over the Dutch door. At the far wall, Niceta nursed while his mother calmly munched strands from the hay bin. She stopped chewing long enough to glance his way, her expression practically demanding an explanation for the rude interruption. Ty ignored her as he probed every inch of the stall.

No child lay on the hay-strewn floor. No small figure huddled in a corner.

Relief whispered through him. It lasted just long enough for him to draw a breath before dread sent icy tentacles down his spine. There were a million ways for a little boy to get hurt on a ranch like the Circle P. Had the kid moved farther into the barn? Climbed into the hayloft? He scanned the wide aisle where doors opened onto twenty empty stalls. No matter how hard he stared, the only motion came from the dust motes glinting in the occasional shaft of sunlight.

"Where is he?"

The voice at his elbow rose perilously. He spared Sarah a quick look. Fear and anger rose off the redhead like smoke from a campfire on a windy day. A sudden desire to take her in his arms and murmur reassuring words swept over him. He shoved the impulse aside. Chances were, she wouldn't appreciate the effort. Not if the sparks in her hazel eyes were any indication.

Thick with accusation, her voice filled the space between them. "What kind of father loses track of his son?"

"I told you, he's not mine." The sharp retort rolled off his tongue before Ty had a chance to marshal enough defenses to hide his own fear.

Sarah reeled as if stunned. "And that means you won't take care of him?" A vigorous shake of her head sent loose curls flying. "I should *never* have brought him here. Connie was right. I should have put him in The Glades."

"That's no place for a child." Steel bands wrapped around Ty's chest at the thought of such a little tyke having to hold his own against much bigger boys.

"It might not be the best place for him, but at least he'd be safe."

"He's safe here. You'll see. He's around here…somewhere." Ty feigned indifference to cover his own concern. Truth was, he was more aware of the potential dangers on the ranch than Sarah could ever be. But losing his cool wouldn't help find the boy and, right now, that was the only thing that mattered.

"Jimmy!" He recalled his dad's no-nonsense tone and mustered a similar one. "Jimmy, where are you?"

"Mister Ty?"

Ty whipped his head in the direction of the yard. Ranch hands and guests mingled just beyond the barn door. Matt Henson and John Padgett walked their horses in circles around their friends. Beyond them, the Garrisons were helping Kelly adjust the stirrups on her new saddle. One of the hands led a horse past the door, blocking Ty's view of the controlled chaos. His fingers clenched. The chances of an accident rose out there where no one would be watching for a mere wisp of a child.

Five of the longest strides he'd ever taken took him to the barn entrance while the bands around his chest tightened until breathing took real effort. He swept the yard with his gaze, his attention zeroing in on a flash of red.

Jimmy's shirt.

The boy, completely safe and apparently unconcerned about the fuss he'd raised, waved from the open front seat of the chuck wagon.

Ty blinked and looked again, needing to be sure his eyes hadn't deceived him. They hadn't.

"See. I told ya everything'd be okay." He glanced down expecting to see his own relief mirrored in Sarah's face. It wasn't, and he braced for her anger.

She spoke through thin lips. "This isn't working. You weren't supposed to let him out of your sight."

"Funny. I must have missed that in the instruction manual." Ty patted his pockets as if he was looking for something. "Oh, that's right. I don't have one. Maybe you should be a little more specific next time you leave him with me."

Sarah's hand found purchase on one slim hip. "Maybe it'd be better for all of us if I took Jimmy back to Fort Pierce. I could probably salvage a few days of my vacation if I tried hard enough."

"You'd do that? Break this kid's heart after you promised he could go on a cattle drive? That's cold, even for a social worker."

The smoke he'd seen rising off her ignited a fire in Sarah's eyes. Whatever. He'd deal with her later. For the moment, he had a more immediate problem. He headed for the five-year-old, determined to impress him with the need for following orders.

"Jimmy, what the— I thought I told you to stay put in the barn. What are you doing out here?"

The boy's wide grin faded. His bottom lip trembled. "I—I..." Jimmy's gaze slid from Ty to the woman at his side.

Sarah's fingers dug into his forearm, and Ty skidded to a halt.

"Don't you dare use that tone with him," she hissed.

Ty got rid of the angry burn, but kept his feet in motion until Seth stepped into his path.

"My fault, boss. I was watchin' him like you said. Didn't mean to cause no trouble."

"Say, what?" Ty hauled up on his hustle, confused by an expression he'd never seen before on his ranch foreman's face.

"Jimmy. The kid."

Seth was clearly trying to convey some secret. What it was, Ty didn't have a clue, but, deciding to play along, he kept his mouth shut.

"You said I should watch out for him while you dealt

with Sad Sack's saddle. I knew you'd be right back, but then Elliot asked about his horse. I just thought Jimmy and me could wait here at the chuck wagon till Doris was ready." He glanced toward the rear of the vehicle where his wife and several ranch hands loaded the last of the supplies and the final two ice chests. "Looks like she's about done."

Ty was willing to bet that however Jimmy had wound up on the buckboard, it didn't have anything to do with Seth. His gaze shifted to the little boy who stared up at him.

"Mr. Ty, did I do something wrong? Are you gonna make me go back?"

Beside him, Ty heard Sarah gasp. Deliberately, he stepped in front of her.

"Back where, little man?"

"Back to Miss Candy." Jimmy's big brown eyes filled with worry far beyond his years. "I don't think she wants me."

Damn it, Millie.

Ty blew out a heavy breath of his own. No sense blaming the dead. He'd probably never know why his ex-wife had named him as this boy's father, but until they found his real dad, it was up to him to fill the breach. To make this kid feel wanted and loved.

"I was just a mite concerned when I couldn't find you, Jimmy, that's all. I'm not sending you anywhere. As long as Miss Sarah here's okay with it, I think we ought to hit the trail. What do you say, Miss Sarah?"

The angry look faded from the petite redhead's face as her focus shifted away from Ty and landed on the boy. Indecision played across her features for long seconds while Ty held his breath and waited. The list of people who had let this kid down was already too long. Would she add to it?

"Let's ride," she said at last. Her lips curved briefly into a warm smile.

Ty caught the look she'd intended for the little boy. As Sarah's features settled back into their normal expression, he realized he'd never really seen her let her guard down. Not completely. Not that she frowned all the time. Her usual expression was just a little bit… He searched for the right word. Stern. She usually looked stern. He wondered how her face would transform if she ever relaxed long enough to enjoy herself.

He rubbed one hand over his chest, glad to feel a slight lessening of the pressure he'd been carrying since he'd caught a glimpse of Sarah as she marched into the house. Her fuming retreat should have irritated him. It probably would have, if she hadn't made wading through deep sand look so sexy.

He let his gaze drift further south. The woman had hidden some serious curves beneath those awful, loose suits he'd dubbed her work uniform. She certainly filled out a pair of jeans better than he'd anticipated. Yes, the sleeveless top exposed too much skin to the sun and the bugs, but he couldn't help but admire her slim arms. As for the way the soft fabric molded her breasts, well…

Ty sucked in a breath.

"You're gonna cover up while we're riding, aren't you?" He nearly bit his tongue knowing he sounded a lot gruffer than he'd intended.

Sarah's eyes hooded. "It's warm out," she said slowly.

Ty clenched his teeth so hard they ached. The woman's sweet curves conjured up images of downy mattresses and candlelight, and he wasn't the only one who'd noticed. John had already shown an interest. Once everyone realized Sarah and Jimmy weren't related, all the other single men on the drive would trip over themselves vying for her attention.

Suddenly feeling a bit overheated himself, he stripped off the long-sleeved flannel shirt he'd pulled on over a plain white T. "Here," he said, thrusting it toward Sarah. "Put this on. Cover your arms and..." *Chest* was the next word, but he couldn't say it. "Sunburn's nothing to fool with."

Sarah left his outstretched hand hanging. "I sprayed myself with sunblock before I left the house.

"As fair as you are, sunblock probably won't be enough. Wear the shirt."

"You won't need it?"

"I'm good." His years on the Circle P made him practically burn-proof. He tried not to stare as Sarah took the proffered shirt and shrugged into it. "If some clouds roll in, you should be okay with just sunblock tomorrow." He might even volunteer to spread the liquid over the freckles that lightly dusted her otherwise creamy white shoulders. Suddenly, the idea of spending the next ten days on a cattle drive didn't seem like such an imposition, not with Sarah along to brighten the view.

Ty bit his tongue. Distance. He needed to put some distance between them before he made an absolute fool of himself.

"Okay, ya'll. Let's mount up and get this show on the road," he called. Across the yard, one of his hands stood holding Ranger's reins. He strode in that direction, giving orders as he went. "Seth, you help Sarah, there, with Belle." He'd chosen the even-tempered mare for her ride. "Doris, you got Jimmy, right?"

"Right, boss." Doris had climbed into the Jeep beside the boy. Even though, strictly speaking, the law didn't require one while they were on private property, she stretched a seat belt across the child's thin frame.

As the riders gathered for their final instructions, Ty counted heads and horses and vehicles, mentally checking items off his list while, in the back of his mind, he pondered ways to bring a full-fledged smile to Sarah's lips by the time they reached the end of the trail.

SARAH SLIPPED HER ARMS into Ty's heavy shirt, rolled the excess cloth to her elbows and tied the dangling ends loosely around her waist. Who would have guessed the big rancher hid so much muscle underneath a pair of long sleeves? Certainly not her. When he'd casually pulled off his shirt, the move had exposed skin that bore a deep, golden tan. Her mouth had gone dry, and she'd stared at the clouds, at the ground, anywhere but at the thin cotton that covered his chest like a glove. Now, with Ty on the far side of the yard, she thought it might be safe to breathe again. She inhaled. Right away she recognized her mistake as a crisp, manly scent filled her lungs. A delicious shiver rippled through her body.

She shook her head.

To say Ty Parker was a puzzle, well, that was an understatement. Whenever she'd met with his college fraternity brothers, Ty had been attentive and caring, seemingly dedicated to providing kids in foster care with the experience of a lifetime. Weeks later, the gruff old bear had marched into her office with not one good word to say about his two charges. And today he'd literally given her the clothes off his back before striding into the distance as if he couldn't get away from her fast enough.

"You ready, ma'am?"

Sarah snapped her focus back where it belonged. She'd sacrificed her vacation to give Ty and Jimmy a chance to get to know one another. Drooling over the man was not part of the job. She exhaled slowly.

"Just a second, Seth. I need to check on Jimmy." She covered the final distance to the chuck wagon. "Are you all set?" she asked the boy.

Despite the restraint across his chest, the child bounced up and down on the seat. "Ms. Doris says we're going to see lots of birds. She's gonna show me some nests later. She said we'd see alligators, too. And snakes."

"Did she now?" Sarah flashed a concerned look at the matronly cook on the seat beside him, but Doris was busy settling a walkie-talkie into a holster glued to the dash and didn't respond. Hoping Jimmy was exaggerating about the wildlife, Sarah pointed to a glossy-coated mare hitched to the post by the corral. "Mr. Seth and I are going to be right over there. You mind Ms. Doris and you call me if you need me."

"Don't you worry about him. We'll have us a good time." Sounding far more tender-hearted than she'd appeared in the kitchen, Doris jiggled the radio once more before she gave Jimmy a quick squeeze. "I've got five of my own—all grown now, of course. It'll be nice to spend some time with a young'un."

Satisfied that Jimmy was in good hands, Sarah followed Seth to the horse Ty had selected for her.

"Her name's Belle." The grizzled foreman nodded at the mare. "She's one of my favorites. Sweet, but with a little spice, if you catch my drift. Don't be afraid to let her know who's the boss."

"Thanks, Seth. She's a beauty." Sarah patted the

mare's long neck. When she scratched between the soft ears, the horse nudged closer. "I'm sure we'll get along just fine. Thanks for earlier, too." She didn't believe for a minute that Ty had tasked Seth with the boy, but no harm had been done. If anything, she thought the rancher had learned a valuable lesson about the vigilance required of parenthood. And that was why she was here, wasn't it? To make sure Ty was well equipped to be Jimmy's dad.

"You need a leg up? Or a stand?" Seth handed her the reins while he aimed a thumb at a nearby mounting block.

"No thanks. I've spent a little time in the saddle." Sarah stepped into the stirrup and swung herself up. Belle shifted slightly beneath her and air fluttered through her lips, but the well-trained horse remained in place. Sarah eased the mare forward and joined the others in a circle around Ty.

"Happy New Year, and welcome to our first midwinter roundup." The owner of the Circle P sat atop a big quarter horse. "Some of you have joined us on our annual summer drive. We're glad to have you back." He nodded to the men he'd introduced as Matt and Elliott. "As you can see, this one is a bit more low-key, but don't worry. Doris'll still whip up her world-famous biscuits every mornin' and serve the best food east of the Mississippi every night."

"Thank goodness," called Matt. "My mouth's been watering for those biscuits for months."

Ty shot Matt a smile while a few chuckles rippled through the gathered riders.

"The herd's about ten miles away, scattered out around Little Lake," he continued. "We'll spend a couple of days there, rounding up about fifty head of cattle a rancher up in the Panhandle wants to add to his stock. Once the vet gives 'em the okay, we'll start the trek to the cow pens in Kissimmee. Everybody okay with that plan?"

When heads nodded, he added, "If you run into a problem, just tell me or Seth. Here on the Circle P, we'll do everything we can to let you experience life like it was a hundred years ago." He grinned. "Well, except there's clean running water and refrigeration. Not to mention the trucks going back and forth between the ranch all the time."

Within minutes, Ty gave the signal that it was time to move out. Whoops and hollers filled the air as guests and ranch hands headed across the grass and scrubland. Erect and holding Belle's reins in the precise manner she'd learned for dressage, Sarah urged the horse toward the chuck wagon where Kelly had already guided her mount next to Jimmy. While the girl pointed out several bird species and quickly engaged the boy in finding new ones, Sarah listened to the youngster's banter.

After seeing that the kids were enjoying themselves, she dropped back. Up ahead, Ty rode with an easy grace, chatting with Matt and his friends. Sarah caught another whiff of Ty's scent as she brushed a wayward hair from her forehead. Ty Parker was a man of many facets, but he definitely needed help to learn how to raise a small boy. And she was just the person to do that, as long as she didn't let herself get too involved.

A trio of sandhill cranes took flight and winged their way across the palmetto not ten yards from where she rode. It wasn't Hawaii, Sarah thought, watching the birds and listening to their hoarse croaking calls, but a trek across Florida might make a good substitute. Some of the tension bled from her shoulders. By the end of the first mile, the jangle of metal and the soft squeak of leather soothed her misgivings about making the trip. The stark beauty of the saw grass and palms, the warmth of the sun on her back worked their magic, and shifting the reins to one hand, she let her wrists drift down toward the pommel like the rest of the riders.

She'd just started to succumb to the mesmerizing sway of the saddle when her cell phone rang. The noise already seemed foreign in the land of palmetto and scrub oak. Recognizing her supervisor's number in the display screen brought a familiar stiffness to her shoulders and Sarah frowned. Connie probably wanted to know why she'd never delivered Jimmy to The Glades.

Sarah shook her head. Sure, she understood the rules. Most of the time, she even agreed with them. But she'd never understand a system that would force a little kid like Jimmy into a group home when he could just as easily stay with someone who cared for him. Knowing she had to decide whether it was a system she could continue to work with, she reached for her phone.

"SO I SAID TO THE GUY, you can't afford *not* to invest with Triple Prime. But he still didn't bite. Man, I tell you, I was sweating bullets. My commission for the entire year rested on this idiot, and I couldn't get him to budge."

Elliott broke in on Matt's story. "Not until the stock market plunged two hundred points the week before Thanksgiving."

"Lot of people lost money that day," Ty said, not really interested but making small talk to keep his guests happy. Fifty years from now, who would know—or care—if the broker had closed the deal?

Matt resettled his hat and squinted in Ty's direction. "You follow the market, do you?"

"Not so much anymore, but I used to. Before I came back to the Circle P, I was a junior partner at Jackson Cole."

"Seriously?" Matt's eyebrows rose at the mention of the elite investment company. "What'd you do there?"

"Handled mutual funds and annuities for the southeast region."

Matt whistled low and under his breath. "You ever want to get back into the business, you just let me know."

Elliott spoke again. "You ought to take him up on it. Matt's great about giving his friends a chance."

Ty took in the beauty of the hammock they were passing through. Moss dripped from sturdy oaks, filtering the sunlight and creating a strobe-light effect he never tired of seeing. "Nah. The view here is better."

Matt flicked his horse's reins. "Well, there is that. But it's worth it when you land a really big account and the commission that goes with it."

For you maybe. But not for me.

He'd had that life once. Even thought it was what he wanted. Coming back to the Circle P, he'd realized how wrong he'd been. It had taken a while, but now he couldn't imagine waking up to an alarm clock instead of the roosters crowing in the henhouse. Except lately, he'd begun to worry about the ranch's future. Parker cattle had grazed on the Circle P for close to a hundred and fifty years. The thought of the land passing into the hands of someone like Ol' Man Tompkins gave Ty a bad case of heartburn. He refused to consider the other alternative—that some developer would snap it up, bulldoze the trees, drain the swamps and erect a city.

The possibility of a child to carry on at the Circle P, now, that would change things.

Ty tipped his hat back and wiped his forehead. When he and Millie were still in the honeymoon phase of their marriage, they'd decided to wait until Ty made full partner before they had a child. If anything, his ex-wife had been even more determined not to have a baby after they moved back to the ranch. He glanced over one shoulder at the chuck wagon. There wasn't much chance she'd changed her mind or that the boy was his.

He drew his hat brim down to shade his eyes while Matt groused about the lengths he'd had to go to bag another wealthy client. His brother Elliott made a good wingman, chiming in as if on cue, pointing out places where a less savvy businessman might have lost the account. Ty waited for a lull in the conversation before he made his excuses and let Matt and Elliott ride on without him. He drifted back, joining the group that followed, exchanging a few words with each of the riders and making sure all his clients were enjoying themselves.

"Ya'll doin' all right?" he asked as he fell in beside Tom and Hope Garrison toward the back of the pack.

"Couldn't be better," exclaimed Tom. "I tell you, the opportunities for bird watching around here are spectacular. You should consider doing more tours specifically geared for birders, like us."

"You think there'd be enough interest?" Ty asked.

"Are you kidding? According to the Audubon Society, birding is the fastest growing sport in North America. Why, thousands attend the annual festival in Brevard County."

Hope raised her binoculars in time to watch a white ibis taking flight. "And Lake Okeechobee is a migratory mecca. Your cattle drive offers the perfect opportunity to see hundreds of species up close, instead of from a tour bus."

"So, I take it you're not really interested in the cows themselves."

"Oh, no," answered Tom. "We're hoping to spot a Smooth-billed Ani." He lowered his own binoculars. "I hope that's okay."

"Hey, whatever makes you happy," Ty said, giving the man and his wife his best aw-shucks grin while he made a mental note to look into Tom's suggestion. In winter, cattle buyers were scarcer than hens' teeth, which made turning the winter roundup into an annual event somewhat difficult. But a birding trail ride? It was definitely worth consideration. He couldn't deny how much he'd welcome another revenue stream for the Circle P.

He listened to Tom and Hope talk about birding for a while before a particular egret caught their attention. As they pulled off the trail, reaching for spiral-bound notebooks and pencils to record the sighting, Ty let the chuck wagon pass by. He waited until Sarah, the last of the trail riders, caught up with him. So far she'd stuck to herself, and he intended to ask if she preferred riding alone. If so, he'd respect her wishes. If not, though... well, he liked to get to know all the guests on his cattle drives, didn't he?

Noting her comfortable seat, he drew in alongside her. "You look like you've done this before a time or two."

"Not since college, but it's all coming back."

"Where'd you go?" Ty asked, aware of the vague

tautness in her smile and wishing he could help her relax.

"Gainesville. Both undergrad and grad school."

"A fellow Gator." He smiled. He'd always associated her reserved manner with an Ivy League education and was surprisingly pleased to learn they'd attended the same state university. "I have my master's in Finance from there."

Sarah hiked an eyebrow above her sunglasses. "What's a guy with a master's degree doing on a cattle ranch?"

"Long story," Ty answered, uncertain whether he was glad for the opportunity to talk about his past with the woman. "I grew up here." He swept his arm through the air in an all-encompassing gesture. Circle P land stretched in every direction for as far as anyone could see and beyond. "Loved it as a kid. Resented it as a teen. Couldn't wait till the day I left for college and said goodbye to my last cow patty."

"A lot of kids want something different from the lives their parents lived," Sarah said softly.

Had it been that way for her? Or had something else led her into social work? When she didn't volunteer the information, he filed his questions away for another time. "That was me. Millie, too. She hated the ranch more than I did."

"So, why'd you come back?"

"Same reason as most, I guess. Dad got sick and there wasn't anyone else—no brothers or sisters. The only other person who could have pitched in was my friend J.D., and he was in the marines. So, I took a leave of absence from my job and moved home to help out. I thought it'd be just for a little while. Till Dad got better.

But things didn't work out that way. The cancer took him quicker than anyone imagined."

"Sorry to hear that," Sarah murmured. After a pause, she asked, "But you stayed on?"

"Yeah. Ranching was in my blood, I guess." He relaxed his grip to give Ranger a little more rein. "Once I'd been back on the Circle P for a while, I knew I didn't ever want to be anywhere else. Millie, she wasn't happy, but I thought she'd get used to it. She proved me wrong by leaving."

He'd thought having J.D. home on leave after his dad died would help. Even though his best friend had argued against his marriage to Millie, the threesome had always been close. And J.D., he'd always been able to make her listen to reason. But if Ty had counted on his friend to smooth things over, he'd been wrong about that, too. Instead, there'd been an added tension in the house that summer. Then, J.D. went to Afghanistan, and before he knew what was happening, there were soldiers in uniform at the door and Millie was packing her bags.

Ty braced himself. It'd been six years since that fateful day, and he still felt his friend's loss as if it'd been last week.

"I can't imagine how awful that must have been for you," Sarah said. "I've never lived through something like that, but I like to think I'd be able to focus on the good that came out of the relationship."

It took Ty a second to realize that Sarah was still talking about Millie. "What good?" he asked.

"Well, there's Jimmy."

Ty stared out over the expanse of grass and palmetto that stretched to the horizon now that they'd left the wooded area behind. In the distance, a dark line smudged the sky, and he cleared his throat.

"We should reach the bunkhouse in another half hour or so," he said, pointing toward the curl of smoke that rose above the chimney. He tipped his hat to Sarah and clucked gently to Ranger. As the quarter horse trotted toward the head of the line, leaving Sarah in the dust, Ty glanced at the kid who, according to her, might be the answer to his concerns for the future.

Chapter Five

"Mmmm nooo." Jimmy moaned and thrashed.

Across the tiny room they shared in the bunkhouse, Sarah pushed her covers aside and swung her legs out of the narrow twin. Floorboards creaked beneath her feet as she moved to the boy's bed where she knelt beside him.

"Shh, sweetheart. It's okay. Everything's going to be all right," she whispered. Freed of its normal restraints, her hair fell around her shoulders. She tucked loose strands behind her ears and continued to make soothing noises.

Bad dreams had disturbed the child's sleep every night since Candy dropped him off at DCF. What troubled him? His past? His future?

Sarah knew very little about the first years of Jimmy's life, but the road ahead was definitely uncertain. If Ty didn't commit to raising him, the boy would probably become a ward of the state. Cute or not, the five-year-old was already too old for most prospective parents. The odds of him ever being adopted were practically nil. In all likelihood, he'd go into the system where he'd bounce from one foster home to another. Few kids escaped such a rootless existence unscathed.

How could Ty let that happen? Even if the child wasn't his flesh and blood, the rancher had been married to Jimmy's mom. Wasn't that alone reason enough to give the boy a home?

She'd do it in a heartbeat, and she had no connection to the boy whatsoever. Sarah stilled. Though she carried a heavy caseload, she couldn't explain why this one child mattered to her more than the others. Jimmy was a sweetheart, but she could name a dozen more just like him. He certainly wasn't the only orphan under her care. But she wanted him to have a home, a family, someone to tuck him in at night and be there when the nightmares troubled his sleep.

Reaching out, she brushed damp hair from his forehead and patted his shoulder.

The boy quieted and rolled over.

Sarah waited until Jimmy's breathing smoothed out before she straightened his blankets, tucking them in around his chin. The comforting sound of his breathing stirred an odd feeling in her chest. She let her hand linger on his shoulder.

Maybe she could adopt him herself.

"Huh!" She shook her head. Assuming she could get past DCF's rule against getting too involved, did she even have what it took to make a good parent? She was on call 24/7. Her job took so much out of her that what little time she had left over, she spent mindlessly gardening. Okay, so maybe a change of environment could fix both ailing flowers and troubled children, but that's about where the similarities ended. If she forgot to water or fertilize a cutting and the plant died, she could always start over. With kids, there were no second chances. If you screwed them up, they stayed that way.

Aware that some of Jimmy's restlessness had rubbed off on her, Sarah tugged a sweatshirt over her pajamas and slipped her feet into scuffs. She eased open the bedroom door and padded down the stairs to the bunkhouse's great room. A light shone through the swinging doors into the kitchen. She followed it to the refrigerator where she helped herself to a glass of milk.

While she sipped, Sarah peered out the window at a group that lingered around the dying campfire. She raised an eyebrow when one of the men—Josh, she thought—took a swig from a bottle and handed it to Tom Garrison. Seth sat on Tom's other side. When the bottle came his way, the older man passed it on without taking a share. A log on the fire collapsed, sending up a shower of sparks. Someone must have told a joke because another round of quiet laughter rippled through the group. She didn't see Ty with the others, and a twinge that was halfway between regret and relief swept through her.

Her milk finished, she set the glass in the sink before she headed back upstairs. No matter what transpired outside, a few more hours of sleep were on her agenda. Ty had said they'd head out at first light and spend the day searching for strays. That meant a full day in the saddle, and she already ached in places that hadn't hurt since the last time she'd ridden a horse, back in her college years.

Sarah was certain her head had barely touched the pillow when small hands gently shook her shoulder.

"Ms. Sarah. Ms. Sarah."

"Good morning." Beneath the covers, she stretched and squinted a smile at Jimmy. The little boy had already dressed for the day in the brand-new jeans and one of several shirts Ty had given him.

"Ms. Sarah, I heared people talking in the hall. I think it's time to get up now."

"You're probably right about that." She spared a quick look out the window. The rising sun had painted gold on the clouds that hugged the eastern horizon. Coffee and other heavenly scents filled the air, and her stomach rumbled. "Something smells good. Give me a second to get dressed and we'll see about breakfast."

By the time Doris banged the triangle that hung from a post outside the kitchen, Sarah and Jimmy had joined the rest of the guests at the buffet table in the main room. There, bowls of grits, hash browns and gravy filled the spaces in between huge platters of bacon and chunks of dark country sausage. Honey, jellies and three kinds of syrup surrounded enormous trays of biscuits and buttery toast.

While Jimmy settled in next to his new best friend, Kelly, Sarah fixed their plates.

"Everybody sleep well?" she asked as she joined the Garrisons at one of the wide trestle tables.

"Nothing like an afternoon of sunshine and fresh air to put me out like a light," answered Hope Garrison. Across the table, her husband downed a couple of aspirin with his coffee. "How about you?"

"Slept like a baby," Sarah said. Her brief foray to the kitchen in the middle of the night didn't merit a mention any more than the small patch of stinging skin just above her neckline. Ty had been right about one thing—the sunburn stung like the dickens.

"Do I have to eat this?" the boy interrupted. He made a face at his plate.

Uncertain of his likes or dislikes, Sarah had chosen a dab of this and a spoon of that from the many breakfast foods. She started to explain. "I thought you might—"

"Got room for one more?"

The deep voice at her shoulder brought a forgiving smile to her lips. Busy playing host to his guests last night, Ty had practically ignored his son at dinner. Breakfast would give them both a chance to get to know one another better.

"Sure," she said, sliding over to make space on the bench. Silverware clattered as Ty placed a towering plate on the table. A shiver passed through Sarah when the rancher's elbow brushed hers. She edged a little farther away, assuring herself, however unsatisfactorily, that she had neither the time or the inclination for an attraction to Ty.

Across the table, Jimmy gave his food a baleful look. "What *is* this stuff?"

"A cowboy's got to start the day with a good meal. Dig in." Ty speared a fat, round sausage with his fork and took a bite.

Looking doubtful, Jimmy poked one finger into his eggs. "I don't like these. What are they?"

"What do you mean—what are they? They're scrambled eggs, little man. They're good for you. Have some." Ty scooped up a mouthful. "You'll like 'em."

Sarah shot the man a warning glance. She'd let Jimmy pick his favorite cereal in the grocery store and hadn't been surprised when he'd chosen something loaded with sugar. Not every child had a Ms. Doris in his life or a mom who started the day off with a hearty breakfast. It would take time for the boy to adjust to the way things were done on the Circle P. Taking the first small step, she worked her way around Jimmy's plate, identifying the foods for him.

"Isn't there any Froot Loops?" The kid tipped his face to hers.

"I saw oatmeal. Would you like some?"

Jimmy made a face.

"Don't you want to grow up big and strong? You gotta eat to do that," Ty grumbled.

This time Sarah skipped the warning look and nudged Ty with her own elbow. She'd come on the cattle drive, in part, to help him develop his parenting skills. That meant learning which battles were worth fighting. She mustered a conciliatory smile for the boy.

"Why don't you try a bite of everything. See what you like and what you don't, and tomorrow you can fix your own plate with all your favorites."

Jimmy snagged the sausage link from his plate and bit into it. "Too spicy," he pronounced. He prodded the mound of grits. "What's that?"

"Ground up corn. You like corn, don't you?" It was the only vegetable the boy would eat.

"It's not yellow." He wiped the granules from his fork. "I like yellow corn."

"Tell you what—you try whatever you want and leave the rest."

Certain the boy wouldn't starve to death, no matter how much or how little he chose to eat, Sarah dug into her own breakfast. She'd sworn she'd never be hungry again after feasting on steak and potatoes the night before, but she couldn't pass up Doris's famed biscuits. As advertised, they were soft and fluffy on the inside with a bit of salty crunch on the outside. Sarah had two and swirled the last one in cane syrup.

Meanwhile, conversation buzzed about the room. Seth stopped by the table and went over the day's plans with Ty. Every once in a while, the rancher glanced across the table at the little boy. He smiled when Jimmy nibbled on a slice of bacon and ate a jelly-smeared biscuit.

At a little after eight, Ty tapped lightly on his juice glass and stood.

"Today, we're going to break into two groups and start rounding up the cattle. The hands have been out this morning scouting the area. The herd's spread out around Little Lake, just like we thought. Mr. and Mrs. Garrison, you, Kelly and Sarah will head east with three or four of the men. Seth and the others'll take the rest of you west. I'll spend the day moving back and forth between the groups in case anyone needs help."

Jimmy looked around, his eyes wide. "What about me, Mr. Ty?"

Sarah held her breath and braced for another clash of wills, but Ty favored the boy with a tight smile. "I heard Ms. Doris say she's making apple pies for supper. She said she was looking for a helper about your size."

The little boy scowled at Sarah. "I want to ride a horse."

Ty's smile lost a little of its wattage. "Tell you what, pardner. You stay here with Ms. Doris. I'll take you for a ride on Ranger after we get back this afternoon."

"Really, Mr. Ty?"

"If it's okay with Ms. Sarah."

Nothing like putting me on the spot, Sarah thought as Jimmy's hopeful eyes searched out hers. Purely for reassurance, she ran a quick look over Ty. Just like him, she, too, needed to pick her battles. "Sure," she said agreeably.

"Okay!"

Sarah's tummy tightened at the goofy grin that sprang onto Jimmy's face. Her heart twisted with a desire to tell the boy yes every time he asked for something. But Ty was talking and she steered their attention back to the man in charge.

"If you get anywhere near the lake, you'll see gators. Don't tease 'em. They move a lot faster than you might think. Last, but not least, watch out for snakes. On a cool day like this, they like to find a nice, sunny spot. As long as you're on your horse, you should be okay, but if you have to dismount for any reason, watch where you're walking."

Ty grabbed his emptied plate and utensils. He started toward the kitchen, but backtracked after a step or two.

"Jimmy, how 'bout you come with me. I'll get you set up with Ms. Doris before I leave."

The little boy scrambled down from his seat.

"Get your plate," Ty admonished, his tone gentle. "On the Circle P, we always clear our place after we eat."

Jimmy kept pace without spilling too much of his leftovers. At the swinging door between the kitchen and the main room, Ty aimed an amused glance in Sarah's direction. She told herself he intended nothing more than to let her know he'd taken her example to heart but, heaven help her, the way his eyes crinkled sent a jolt right through her. Her mouth went dry. She reached for her water glass, not that it did any good. It'd take more than water to cool her growing attraction to the rancher.

An attraction she was determined to ignore, she told herself. She was here for a purpose—to see what kind of home Ty would make for Jimmy. That didn't include making goo-goo eyes at the man.

TY SHEPHERDED JIMMY THROUGH the door and into the kitchen. At the large garbage cans that stood beside the back door, he showed the kid how to scrape his plate and gave himself points for not cringing at the amount of food the boy tossed into the trash.

"Tomorrow," he said, "don't take anything you won't eat. Okay, pardner?"

"I like biscuits," Jimmy announced. "And bacon."

"Well, now, that's fine. Mighty fine. Now then, let's go turn you over to Ms. Doris."

The two young men washing pots and pans motioned him out back. He found the cook at a picnic table under a spreading oak tree, an ice chest on the ground at her feet, a large bowl in her lap.

"Any problems, Ty?" she asked without bothering to get up.

And no wonder. Doris was usually working on her second cup of coffee by the time he wandered through the kitchen on his way to the barn in the mornings.

"Another superb breakfast." Ty rubbed his flat stomach.

The fatigue lines etching Doris's face shifted into grandmotherly wrinkles. She patted the bench beside her. "Jimmy, I hear you're going to be my helper today."

Thankful she'd taken the initiative, Ty relinquished his hold on the young boy's shoulder.

Jimmy remained where he was, his feet planted. "I want to ride a horse, but Mr. Ty said I can't. Not till later."

"On a ranch, everybody has to do their share." Doris gave the boy a half smile and a knowing look. "We'll have some fun, too. Grab me another bag of beans out of that ice chest and sit here beside me. You can start right now by helping me get these ready to cook for supper. Have you ever snapped beans before?"

"No." Jimmy stepped close enough to peer into her bowl. "They're green. Do I have to eat them?"

"You don't have to. But these'll be so good, I bet you'll want a whole bowl all for yourself." At Jimmy's dubious look, she laughed. "Not fond of vegetables, huh? That's okay. It means there'll be more for me. You run and wash your hands and then we'll sit and snap a spell."

"He seems to like you," Ty said when the kid darted toward the kitchen. A hint of longing twisted his insides. "How'd you get so good with him?"

"Years of practice," Doris answered. She flipped her long braid over her shoulder with the back of one hand. "There was a passel of boys around here once upon a time. You and J.D. were only two of them."

For a moment, only the sound of a mockingbird in the treetop broke the silence.

Ty cleared his throat. "You think he's mine?"

Doris looked into the doorway where the child had disappeared. "He's got Millie's cheekbones, her fine features, that's for sure. Is he yours? Can't rightly answer that. You took a blood test."

The statement didn't require a response. Ty gave one anyway. "Yep. Won't get the results for another week or two."

Doris plunged her fingers into the bowl and swiftly snapped a handful of the long thin pods into pieces. "Till you know for sure, it won't do either of you any good if you get too attached to that boy. Not unless you're planning to keep him."

Wise advice and exactly what he'd been thinking but had been unable to put into words. Determined to keep his distance from the kid, Ty tempered his smile as Jimmy rushed back, his hands still dripping wet.

"I'm ready now, Ms. Doris."

Doris shooed Ty along while she drew the boy onto the bench beside her. "Okay, now this here is easier than the pies we're gonna make later. First, you take one of these pods, like this..."

The cook's voice faded. Doris would have the boy snapping beans like he'd been doing it all his life before Ty even reached the paddock. When he rode back into camp tonight, there'd be apple pies made by Jimmy's two little hands. Of that Ty had no doubt.

How he felt about it, now that was a question.

He'd dreamed of having children of his own. But he had to admit he knew far more about cattle and horses than little boys. Jimmy presented an unexpected opportunity to expand his knowledge. Sure, the kid probably wasn't his, but who was to say he couldn't learn the ropes of parenting as long as the boy was on the Circle P?

Ty mulled the option over without finding a downside. As long as no one got too close or too involved, it seemed like a win-win situation. He'd see that Jimmy had the time of his life on the ranch. Make sure the boy socked away enough memories to sustain him until Sarah located his real father. In the meantime, Ty would pick up some parenting skills that might come in handy...one day. He didn't have to look far to find expert advice. Doris knew practically everything there was to know about young'uns. Sarah, too. And having the social worker show him how to relate to the child might even be fun.

Ty clamped his hat on his head and strode toward the hitching post. Sarah was definitely easy on the eyes, especially now that she'd traded in those awful business suits for tight-fitting jeans and a cowboy hat. But the woman was simply wound too tight to be his cup of joe. Not that he was looking for a relationship, casual or otherwise.

DELAYED BY HER OWN NEED for reassurance that Jimmy and Doris were set for the day, Sarah double-checked the girth strap and the placement of Belle's bit just as Seth and his group rode out of the yard. She rubbed a hand over the hard saddle and sighed. Behind her, the jangle of metal and the squeak of leather signaled the arrival of another rider.

"Something wrong?" From atop Ranger, Ty eyed her quizzically.

Sarah shook her head. "No. Just wishing there was a bit more padding. After yesterday, I wouldn't mind tying a soft pillow or two over that saddle."

The rancher chuckled. "The first couple of days can be a bit hard on the, uh...derriere," he finished with a teasing smile.

Sarah wrenched her gaze away from an appreciative gleam that made her heart race. White birds wheeled against the cloudless blue sky over miles of palmetto and pines. Beyond them, she glimpsed a shimmer of water. Spotting a trio of riders on horseback in the distance, she shaded her eyes. "I thought the Garrisons were with us today? Where are they headed?"

Ty swung around so his gaze followed Sarah's. "They wanted to do a little birding away from the rest of the group. Said they'd meet up with us at lunch."

Her legs and thighs protesting, Sarah fit her foot into the stirrup and swung onto Belle. "So, it's just you and me?" The prospect of spending several hours alone with Ty was far more intriguing than she thought it should be.

"Unless that's a problem. Josh and a couple of the others got a head start on us. We'll catch up with them."

"No. It's okay."

Ty touched a heel to Ranger's side. The horse moved forward over the flat land, seeming to know his way around the thick patches of palmetto, his hooves leaving deep imprints in the gray sand. Belle's reins in one hand, Sarah urged the mare to walk alongside the other horse.

"Actually, there's something I wanted to say to you, and it'll be easier if we're by ourselves." Sensing this was as good a moment as any, she plunged ahead.

"I think I owe you an apology."

"You think?" Ty canted his head, peering at her from beneath the brim of a cowboy hat. "Or you know?"

"Can you settle for a maybe?"

When he chuckled and nodded, she continued. "I came downstairs last night. There were still people around the campfire. Someone had a bottle, and everyone was helping themselves."

"Everyone?" Ty's broad shoulders edged back a notch.

"Well, no. Seth was there, but he wasn't drinking."

"Good. He said he'd keep an eye on things." The sudden tension in Ty's voice eased. After a pause, he added, "Same as always."

"I'm just saying it was a far cry from the wild parties Chris and Tim talked about."

They moved into a stand of pines that smelled of evergreen and tree sap. A thick bed of needles covered the dirt. Beneath the horses' hooves, fallen branches crackled and popped. Ranger snorted.

"What you saw last night, that's about as crazy as it ever gets at the Circle P. My men and I, we don't abide heavy drinking. A hungover cowboy just isn't much good on a ranch."

"Well, if that's the way it is, I'm sorry for yelling at you about Chris and Tim. It sounds like they exaggerated a bit."

Beyond the wooded copse, ranch hands spread out across the open land. While they herded cattle by ones or twos from thickets of palmetto and brush, Ty pulled Ranger to a halt under a pine tree. He leaned forward, his arms crossed so his weight rested on the pommel. "Can't blame you for protecting those boys. I imagine there are just as many instances where the stories kids tell are true."

Sarah gave her head a rueful shake. "You wouldn't believe it." There were way too many bad people in the world. DCF did its best to weed them out, but every so often someone who shouldn't have anything to do with children slipped into the system. Often, her first indication of a problem came from the kids themselves. So, she'd learned to listen when they talked. Before Ty had a chance to respond to her explanation, movement in the bushes just beyond the clearing drew her attention. She pointed.

"If I'm not mistaken, there's a cow behind that stand of palmetto up ahead."

Ty leaned forward and scanned the thick brush. "Good eye. We'll make a cowgirl out of you yet. Why don't you circle 'round to the left. I'll take right, and we can ease her on out."

Slowly, she moved Belle into position. They stepped from beneath the trees, dry grass rustling under the horses' hooves. When Ty removed his hat, Sarah did the same. They worked as a team, moving forward while Ty swung his arms and called, "Hey-hey-hey now. Come on out, gal."

The wide palmetto fans rustled. Sarah and Ty tightened their circle until, at last, a mottled face topped by short, curving horns broke from the bushes. The sleek, brown cow trotted away from them, her hooves plodding heavily against the dirt. Watching Ty, Sarah waited until their quarry slowed to a walk before she guided Belle alongside Ranger.

"You did that like you've been rounding up cattle your whole life," Ty said.

The simple praise warmed Sarah's face. She tugged her own hat down low over her eyes and offered a sincere, "Thanks, but I have no idea what we do next."

"That part's simple," Ty said with an easy assurance. "All we do now is follow along, slow-like, until we meet up with the others. We'll gather together seven or eight head, then slowly move them toward the pens. The cattle know the way 'cause when the weather's cold or the grass dies back, we drop feed off there."

It would be easy to succumb to Ty's personality, Sara realized. The rancher had a generous nature, a ready smile she could get used to. But she'd come to the Circle P for Jimmy's sake and, taking a deep breath, she turned their conversation to the boy.

"Makes you wish kids were as easy to handle, doesn't it?"

The humor fell from Ty's face. His lips straightened into a thin line. "What was all that about at breakfast? Millie never was much for mornings, but I can't believe she never scrambled an egg for the boy. Or fried up a rasher of bacon."

Sarah shrugged. She'd removed children from homes where refrigerators held nothing more than cheap beer and a bottle of ketchup. "From what Candy said when she dropped him off, money was tight."

"Now, see, that's what doesn't make any sense. Millie dreamed big. A house in the city was at the top of her list. If this kid really is mine, she would've asked for support."

The conversation had wandered onto a treacherous patch of ground. But with Jimmy's best interests at stake, Sarah forced herself to ask the tough questions. "What kind of relationship did you have with her? Was she faithful?"

"Are you asking if my wife cheated on me? Six weeks ago, I'd have said no. I'm not saying my life with Millie was a picnic. That year after we moved back to the Circle P wasn't the best time for us." Ty cleared his throat. "The ranch was bleeding money and, for a while there, I thought the banks were gonna foreclose. It took working around the clock seven days a week to save the place. By then, she was gone."

As they rode through a patch of grass, their cow veered off the path. Ty slapped his reins against Ranger's neck, urging the horse to one side and leaving Sarah to wonder if she'd ventured too far into the rancher's personal life. But no, she decided when he swung in beside her after they were once more headed in the right direction. He just needed a minute to get his thoughts together.

"Any chance you could ask this Candy person more about their time in New York? See if she wants to raise the boy?"

Not liking where Ty's thoughts had taken him, Sarah suppressed a groan. He was no closer to acknowledging Jimmy as his son than he had been when they'd met in her office two days earlier.

"I think we've seen the last of Miss Candy Storm." Though it didn't matter—Ty was Jimmy's father—Candy hadn't called once to check on the boy. Sarah's calls went straight to voice mail. Not one had been returned.

"Too bad," Ty murmured. "I sure would like to ask her a few questions. See if Millie confided in her."

That sounded more like the way Ty should be thinking, but before Sarah had a chance to comment on it, they'd reached Josh and his band of riders. After checking in, Ty brushed two fingers past his hat brim.

"I have to go check on the others now. I'll catch up with you later."

Sarah tried not to feel abandoned as the man rode away. He'd said from the beginning he needed to split his time between the two groups of wranglers, and he had spent quite a while talking with her. Still, as she watched him go, she couldn't help wondering what it'd be like to have someone like Ty around all the time.

Chapter Six

Sarah wrenched her gaze from Ty's broad shoulders as he rode away. When her thoughts refused to budge from the handsome rancher, she gave herself a stern lecture. Much as she wanted what was best for Jimmy, she hadn't come to the Circle P to dwell on the boy's reluctant father. She'd intended to use her vacation to sort out her feelings about her job and make plans for the future.

Well, there was no time like the present.

Urging Belle forward, she ignored the rustle of green palmetto fronds brushing against the horse's flanks and focused on the problem. She'd been promised Connie's job when the woman retired. As director of the Fort Pierce office, she'd be able to implement the changes needed to better serve the children in foster care. Only, the longer Sarah worked with Connie, the more her boss refused to set a departure date, and that was a problem. Worse, every improvement Sarah suggested earned her another black mark in Connie's little book. Add in the bureaucracy, politics and impossibly long hours and there was only one logical conclusion. Though she'd invested seven years in changing the system, the only thing that had changed was her…and not for the better. She had to leave DCF.

And go where? There wasn't much call for former social workers. Gardening was her only other marketable skill. But was her love of tropical plants enough?

While she searched for cows hidden in the thick brush, Sarah examined ideas for turning her hobby into a money-making business. Within an hour, she had the beginnings of a plan. One that might pay her a salary while she changed the environment of one child at a time.

Satisfied that she'd taken a positive step toward the future, Sarah guided another wayward cow into the small herd of eight or nine the others had gathered. By the time Josh waved his hat, signaling the time to head back to camp, she looked forward to sitting on something other than hard leather and a moving horse. She clucked to Belle just as a soft buzzing sounded from her hip.

Sarah whipped her cell phone from her pocket. When her boss's name appeared on the screen, she cupped one hand over the speaker.

"You go on, Josh. I'll catch up."

"Sarah, we're having…with the new…system. What's your…" Connie's voice faded in and out.

"I'm sorry. I didn't quite get that." Sarah glanced over her shoulder at the sandy mound she'd passed ten minutes earlier. Hoping for better reception there, she urged Belle into a trot and headed away from the rest of the riders.

"What's your…"

"Hold on. Let me move to a spot where I can hear you better," Sarah shouted over a rush of wind and clomping hooves.

Startled, Belle sidestepped and blew air through her nostrils. Though Sarah reined to the left, she only succeeded in turning them in a small circle.

"C'mon, girl," she coaxed, but the horse had apparently decided to show a bit of the spunk Seth had mentioned.

Again, Sarah tried to get them going in the right direction, and again Belle balked.

"We need…word."

Unable to battle a willful horse and respond to her boss's demands at the same time, Sarah dismounted. She looped the reins over the closest palm frond and stalked the rest of the way to the mound that was little more than a wide patch of gray sand. There, marginally better reception enabled her to hear well enough to answer Connie's questions about passwords for the new computer system.

"How are Mr. Parker and the boy getting along?" her boss asked minutes later.

"Ty—the dad—is still coming to grips with the idea that he has a five-year-old," Sarah reported. "But they're making progress."

Her fingers crossed, she turned to watch the small herd of cattle cross the open plain. They'd almost reached the copse of woods where she and Ty had found their first cow. Soon, the small band would be out of sight. Sarah sighed. Apparently, they'd be taking Belle with them. Her reins dragging the ground, the horse trotted back the way they'd come.

"Damn," Sarah whispered. It was a long walk back to camp in a new pair of boots that pinched her feet.

"Connie, I have to go now." She punched the button, disconnecting the call. The moment she lowered the phone to her waist, a harsh rattle rose above the gentle whir of cicadas and the rustle of palm fronds. Sarah glanced in the direction of the sound. She froze.

Stretched out on the sand not ten feet from her boots lay the biggest rattlesnake, the only rattlesnake, she'd ever seen that wasn't in an enclosure at the zoo.

"Double damn," she whispered.

TY SPOTTED A CLOUD OF DUST. He shaded his eyes and studied the cattle and riders. Josh and his crew had spread out in a loose semicircle around a small herd of prime Andalusians. As they headed his way in no particular hurry, Ty swept the group a second time, letting his gaze linger on each rider. An odd feeling tickled the back of his throat the second he realized Sarah wasn't among them. He fought the urge to kick Ranger into a cow-scattering gallop. Instead, he gave the horse a soft tap. His pace steady, he rode straight for the man he'd left in charge.

"Looks like you lost one," he said, reining in beside Josh.

The young man's eyes narrowed to a squint. "Nope. We gathered up fifteen head. All accounted for."

"What about Sarah?" Ty prompted. "Didn't you lose her somewhere along the way?"

Josh aimed a thumb over his shoulder. "No, boss. She said she had business to attend to and we should go on ahead. I think she got a phone call."

With Josh's chin tucked into his neck and his hat brim pulled low, Ty couldn't stare into the ranch hand's eyes the way he wanted. He let his voice drop into a deeper register. "So you just left her out there…alone?"

"We let those bird watchers go off on their own this morning. What's the diff?"

"I shouldn't have to point that out to you." Sure, the

Garrisons had separated from the roundup, but there'd been three of them. If one got hurt, the others could ride for help.

On her own, Sarah was vulnerable.

When Josh swallowed so visibly that his Adam's apple bobbed up and down, Ty dialed back his anger. Not even a greenhorn like Sarah could get lost on the flat prairie. Behind him, smoke rose from the big wood-burning stove in the bunkhouse. She couldn't miss the dark smudge against the sky.

"You want me to go back and get her?"

"Nope." Ty waved the boy off. Josh had been asking for more responsibility lately, and he'd given him a chance. But, clearly, the young man wasn't ready to take charge of their guests. Not yet. "My fault. I'll handle it."

He turned away, thankful no one could see the worry that tugged at the corners of his mouth. As he led Ranger over grass trampled by the herd, he realized putting the kid in charge hadn't been his only mistake. The Circle P offered its guests the chance to experience a different way of life, and, in his mind, that meant leaving the gadgets back at the ranch.

He shook his head. Yesterday, when she'd reached for her phone he hadn't missed the way Sarah's demeanor had instantly shifted from open and friendly to tense and anxious. Before she'd pressed a single button, her shoulders had squared and her eyes had hardened. That call had been work-related, and her reaction made him wonder why she'd chosen such a tough profession in the first place.

Did she come from a broken family? Had she spent time in foster care as a youngster?

Whatever her background, she wasn't all straight-laced and uptight. Not like he'd expected her to be. In fact, when she let her hair down, she could be downright fun. But the image of Sarah's hair cascading around her shoulders made him think of running his fingers through the fine, silky strands. From there, he was only one small step away from pulling her close and tasting her lips. A not-unpleasant fullness stirred below his waist at what might come next. The touch of smooth skin. The light scrape of nails across his back. Whispered conversations in the middle of the night.

Ty straightened. He'd given his heart away once already, to a woman he'd known far longer than he'd known the slim social worker, and look where that had gotten him. Divorced and in danger of raising a kid who wasn't his. Only a fool would fail to see how attached Sarah had become to Jimmy. She'd never understand how he could turn his back on the child.

Two people with such wildly differing viewpoints had no business in a relationship.

No, he wasn't looking for anything more than friendship from Sarah. Or any other woman for that matter. His life on the Circle P kept him busy enough, too busy to find someone special and build a relationship. Yes, he'd admit he sometimes regretted not having someone to come home to after a long day of mending fences or feeding cattle, but his one attempt at marriage hadn't worked out so well. Maybe one day he'd try again, but right now a wife and family weren't in the cards he'd been dealt.

Something rustled in the bushes off to Ty's right. He glanced up from the hoofprints he'd been tracking, prints that led him away from the path the herd had taken. Had he stirred up the local wildlife? All manner of animals called the grazing land home. Some weren't all that friendly. Though the predators usually prowled at night, he half hoped for a glimpse of an endangered panther. A wild boar or bobcat were more likely and, one hand on his rifle butt, he waited while something moved through a thick stand of pepper trees.

What the—

Ty swore softly. Whatever he'd expected, a riderless and winded Belle was the last thing he wanted to see. The mare trotted toward him, weaving her way through the palmettos.

Where was Sarah?

Despite a tight feeling in his gut, Ty calmly picked up the horse's reins and looped them around his saddle horn. A quick scan of the mare's tack reassured him that everything was right where it was supposed to be…except for her rider. The muscles across Ty's stomach drew taunt.

"Where is she, girl?" he muttered.

He whipped a pair of binoculars from his saddlebag. When he focused in on the area where he expected to find Sarah, his heart leaped into his throat.

The woman stood, statuelike, in the center of a small clearing.

Snakes. Had to be.

A gator would have charged long ago. A hog would have brought her down in an instant.

His hand hovered over the rifle in its scabbard. Reluctantly, he left it where it was. Television and movies to the contrary, making a clean shot from a moving horse was nearly impossible. He'd be far more likely to hit the girl than the snake. And that was a chance he couldn't take. There was only one thing to do and, no matter what the consequences, Ty told himself he had no choice.

Sarah's life came first. Even if it meant putting Ranger's at risk.

Leaving Belle to her own devices, he slowly rode toward the clearing.

"Easy now," he whispered when Ranger stopped and pawed the ground. Together, they'd run across enough snakes for Ty to know the horse wouldn't bolt. That didn't mean the quarter horse was happy to enter the immediate vicinity of a sunbathing diamondback. Ten feet long and thicker than Ty's upper arm, the rattler stretched across the sand just beyond the spot where Sarah stood, frozen.

He patted Ranger's neck. "I see it, too, but we gotta get the girl."

The big horse blew a forceful breath but kept moving. One hoof at a time, Ranger took them closer until Ty saw the fear—bright and glassy—in Sarah's eyes. He signaled her to remain still. His focus on the snake, he watched for any sign the beast might coil and strike while he positioned the horse between it and Sarah.

The tip of the snake's tail twitched. A warning rattle sounded. Beneath him Ty felt Ranger quiver. Leaning down, Ty wrapped his hands around Sarah's waist.

"On three," he whispered. "One. Two."

He lifted while she practically leaped into his arms. In one smooth move, he settled her sideways in front of him. Her arms curled around his neck. Holding her close, Ty let Ranger have his lead. Once the horse put a safe distance between them and the clearing, Ty risked a quick look over his shoulder. The snake had disappeared leaving a wide track in the sand as the only sign of the danger they'd faced.

Now that they were safe, he let fear and anger overtake him.

"What on earth were you thinking?"

Sarah's muffled voice rose from the face she'd buried in his shoulder. "I was trying to take a call. Belle wouldn't go where I wanted."

"And no wonder. She knew the snake was there. You were damn lucky that rattler didn't coil, didn't strike."

In his arms, he felt shivers course up and down Sarah's spine. The reality of how scared she'd been struck home. He felt sick to his stomach for yelling. She'd always seemed so strong and sure of herself. This vulnerability was unexpected. He didn't know quite how to handle it, so he did the only thing that came to mind. He wrapped his arms around her and drew her close.

"Sorry," he mumbled. They rode for a while before she stopped shaking and her hands thawed. "You okay?" he asked at last.

"Yeah." The fingers she'd threaded through his hair curled into themselves as if she'd suddenly realized what she was doing. She pulled away from him, taking the warmth of her body with her. "I think I can ride by myself now," she whispered.

"Yeah, yeah, okay," he agreed, though he wanted nothing more than to hold her in the shelter of his arms.

He dismounted. He was only keeping her safe—or so he told himself—as he helped her down from her perch atop Ranger. But the brush of her body against his sent a current straight through him. He heard the sharp intake of her breath, saw the slight widening of her eyes and knew she felt the same thing. She'd lost her hat somewhere along the way. Wisps of hair had fallen into her face. With the barest touch, he brushed them from her forehead.

"Sarah?" he whispered.

Her face flushed, but her voice remained firm and

unshakable. "I think we'd better get back to the others, don't you?"

Ty's hands dropped from her waist. He stepped back to put some distance between them.

"It's about time for lunch," he said, regaining control. "We'll head back to camp."

He remounted Ranger while Sarah turned toward Belle. But all the way back to the camp he couldn't stop thinking about how well she'd fit in his arms and how cold and empty they felt without her.

IN THE LUNCH line an hour later, Sarah swallowed past the lump that formed in her throat every time she thought of how close she'd come to being bitten. She placed a hand over her heart and felt a wave of relief that it still beat within her chest. Spotting Ty at one of the tables, she grimaced, this time because one look at the rancher sent her pulse into overdrive. Okay, so riding off into the wilds of South Florida on her own hadn't been her smartest move. And getting down off of Belle without checking the area for snakes or other wildlife had bordered on insanity. But having the big, strong rancher rescue her had been almost as dangerous. No doubt he'd kept her safe, but was her heart now at risk?

She hadn't meant to bury her fingers in his thick hair, hadn't intended to snuggle so close to his chest that the ragged thud of his heartbeat filled her ears. But she had. Of course, he'd just saved her life, so maybe it was natural to feel drawn to him.

Yeah, right. You just keep telling yourself that.

The truth was, she'd been fighting an attraction to the rancher since the first time she met him. She'd staved it off by hauling out all the usual arguments. The man was too opinionated, didn't know a thing about kids, wouldn't even acknowledge his own son. Still, she'd been shocked when he'd held her. She hadn't expected to feel so safe, so secure wrapped in his arms. For one long, wonderful moment, she'd wanted to stay pressed against his chest forever.

And then, she'd regained her sanity. Only, she'd backed away so quickly she was certain she'd given him the wrong impression.

So, what was she going to do about it?

The line shuffled forward. Doris ladled thick Brunswick stew into Sarah's bowl.

"Thanks." She fought back a frown. Though the stew smelled divine, she wasn't sure how she'd manage to swallow a single bite. The opportunity to be embraced by strong, male arms didn't come along often. For it to happen the same day she came within ten feet of possible death, well, both had stolen her appetite along with her breath.

The best thing, the safest thing, was to avoid all such occurrences in the future. She studied the tall man who spoke with Seth on the opposite side of the room. Unless she intended to pack up and leave, avoiding Ty for the rest of the journey would be impossible. Especially when she longed to feel the rancher's arms around her again.

Her thoughts bouncing in too many directions, she grabbed a wedge of corn bread from a serving tray before taking a second one for the boy beside her.

"Ms. Doris and I fixed the beans for supper tonight. Did you know if you break beans, they pop like a firecracker? Only Ms. Doris says they snap. She calls 'em snap beans."

Sarah stared down at the little boy whose New York

accent had already softened. Another week or two on the ranch and he'd sound Southern born and bred. Just like his dad.

"I washed the tomatoes for the salad, but Ms. Doris says I don't have to eat it. And I took all the pickles out of their jars and put 'em in the big dishes. Then we made cob-cob-cobbler. Aren't you going to have some? I sprinkled the stuff on top."

Sarah managed to grasp Jimmy's hand an instant before his fingers poked into the crust of the big dessert pan.

"You did a very good job." She spooned a small portion of berries and crunchy topping onto her plate and dished up a larger helping for the boy. "What are you and Ms. Doris doing this afternoon?"

Jimmy carried his tray to a vacant table. "We're gonna make pies. I like pie. Chocolate is my favorite, but Ms. Doris says we're gonna make apple."

"Mmm. I like apple." Sarah wondered if she'd be hungry by then. She glanced down at Jimmy's tray. The boy had slathered a pound of butter over a thick slice of bread. His bowl, though, was empty. She tipped hers, offering some of her own.

"Nmmmf," he said around the mouthful of corn bread he'd stuffed in his mouth. Something equally unintelligible followed.

Sarah pointed to Jimmy's glass of milk and suggested he take a sip.

"No, thanks," he said when he'd swallowed. "Mr. Ty said I hav'ta eat whatever's on my plate."

Sarah reluctantly dipped her spoon into the bowl. If Jimmy was taking the rancher's advice to heart, hungry or not, she guessed she'd have to follow the rules. Fortunately, the stew tasted as good as it smelled. She was scraping the last of the delicious broth from her bowl when Ty stood to address the group.

"If I could have your attention before we head out again this afternoon." While conversations trailed off and the clatter of silverware stilled, Ty removed his hat and brushed his hair away from his forehead. "Ya'll know we want you to experience a different way of life while you're at the Circle P, one your grandparents might have lived. However, no one wants you to put your lives in danger. But that's what happened this morning when one of our guests had a run-in with a diamondback rattler."

The room went deathly still except for Hope Garrison who gasped, "Was anyone hurt?"

"No, ma'am." Ty spun his hat by the brim.

As his gaze drifted across the gathering of ranch hands and guests, Sarah felt her heart stutter. She'd known from the beginning that forgiveness didn't play a big role in Ty's vocabulary. For proof, she only had to look at the way he'd treated Chris and Tim. Snuggled against his chest as he carried her to safety, she hadn't given a single thought to the possibility that he'd use her mistake against her. Watching him now, though, she knew he was only minutes away from aiming an accusatory finger at her and pointing out how foolish it had been to wander off on her own. She braced herself for a scathing rebuke while Ty scanned the room.

"The weather's turned a might cool and the snake was so busy sunning himself he didn't want to be bothered, but next time, we might not be as lucky, so ya'll take care out there. Okay?"

Her throat taut, Sarah nodded along with everyone else.

"From now on, I'd like to make sure one of our ranch

hands stays with all our guests whenever they leave the camp." Ty aimed a glance at the Garrisons. "Hope, Jim, Seth'll assign someone to go with you this afternoon if you want to do some more birding."

Sarah saw the glimmer of fear in the look Hope shared with her husband. Tom cleared his throat. "No need," he said to his wife's obvious relief. "We'll stick with everyone else."

Ty nodded. "Well, then, that's all I had to say. Whenever you're ready, ya'll can mount up. We'll try to round up another group of cattle this afternoon and tomorrow. Just remember, wherever you are, whatever you're doing, be careful."

Relieved that Ty hadn't raked her over the coals, Sarah tugged her bottom lip between her teeth. Every time she thought she had him figured out, he did something totally unexpected. And now that he'd shown his kinder nature, keeping her guard up around him was going to be even more of a challenge. Especially when she'd decided that facing another snake wouldn't be so bad if it meant riding off in Ty's arms.

Chapter Seven

"Sarah, you want to hand him up?"

With dinner out of the way, Ty had run out of excuses. It was time to make good on the promise he'd given Jimmy that morning, the one the little rascal had been hounding him about ever since.

Ty reached down from Ranger's saddle. As he grasped Jimmy's waist, his hands brushed Sarah's. The tiny jolt that usually coursed through him whenever he touched her struck again. He gave her his best, reassuring look.

"Don't worry. We'll be fine."

Sarah's bland expression was difficult to decipher. Her "I'm sure *he* will be" was so hard to fathom that Ty would have scratched his head if it hadn't meant dropping a very excited five-year-old. He'd have sworn the attraction he'd felt as he held her in his arms hadn't been one-sided, but ever since she'd backed away from their near-kiss, Sarah had given him the cold shoulder.

Women. He'd never understand 'em.

At least he was on to some of Sarah's ways, no matter how hard she'd tried to fool him. He knew she hoped he'd develop such close ties to Jimmy that he wouldn't be able to give the boy up when the paternity tests proved what he'd been saying all along—that he wasn't this kid's dad. But she was in for a shock. He wouldn't let himself get that close to the child. Once the results came in, she'd have to start looking for the boy's real dad. And then Jimmy and Sarah would disappear from his life.... Just like Millie had.

He wrenched his thoughts away from the past and lifted the dangling kid high into the air. At the sound of boyish giggles, Ty leaned forward and ruffled the kid's hair. But when he clucked to Ranger and the horse started forward, Jimmy fell as silent as a tombstone. Not one word passed his lips for the entire five minutes it took to make a slow circuit around the yard.

"You having fun?" Ty asked, concerned. The little boy in his arms was as thin as a bird and his bones felt just as fragile.

Jimmy tipped an awe-filled face up to his. "Mr. Ty," he said, his eyes wide. "This is the best day ever."

Ty blinked. It killed him that the kid—Millie's son—had reached the advanced age of five without ever sitting in a saddle. Riding a horse was just a part of life on the Circle P. He wanted more for the boy than a couple of loops around the yard. He wanted to make the occasion truly special. They'd gone around twice more when he bent low over the boy.

"Now, pardner, you handled that so well, I think you're ready for the next step. See here, this here's how you hold the reins." Ty demonstrated, showing the boy the same way his father had taught him. "You think you can do that?"

"Yeah," Jimmy breathed. He reached for them.

"Use your other hand," Ty corrected. He showed the boy how to leave his stronger arm free for important work.

They tried again, and this time, Jimmy did just fine.

"Like this, Mr. Ty?" Jimmy held out his hands.

"Perfect." Ty had been so young he didn't remember the first time his dad let him hold the reins, but Jimmy seemed to be a bright young boy. If someone took the time to teach him, he'd catch on quickly. "Okay now, tug a little bit to the left."

While Ranger stood still, Jimmy pulled to the right.

Ty scowled. "The other way, boy. Don't you know your right from your left?"

"No. What is it?"

Wondering when kids learned such things led to questions Ty didn't want to ask. Questions like how many hours a day Jimmy spent in front of the television and had Millie devoted any time at all to teaching the boy things a child needed to know. He touched the kid's shoulder. "This is your left side." Gently, he pressed the boy's other arm. "And this is your right. Now, try tugging to the left."

Ty pressed his knee to Ranger's side just as Jimmy gave the leather straps a tentative pull. A horse as well-trained as Ranger responded to both leg and rein commands, and the big head swung to the side.

"See, that's how you tell him which way to go. You pull on the reins. Now, let's go to the right."

Jimmy gave another pull while Ty signaled the horse again. The boy giggled.

"Okay, now we're gonna take another walk around the yard, but this time you tell Ranger which way you want him to go." Ty lightly placed his hands on his thighs, ready to catch the kid if he started to tumble. He needn't have bothered. With Ranger responding to his knee commands, they took another loop around the yard.

"Can I ride him by myself, Mr. Ty?"

"We might want to start you off with something a little closer to the ground. Ranger's a big horse for a big rider. Someone my size. You grow a bit more and we'll see what we can do." He forced himself to ignore the voice in the back of his head that reminded him Jimmy wouldn't be on the Circle P by the time the kid grew tall enough to handle a full-grown horse.

Ty let Jimmy ride until color faded from the western sky. Though they'd stayed within the perimeter of the camp, beyond it animals had begun to stir. Squeaks filled the air as clouds of bats rose from the palm trees to fly in search of mosquitoes. From somewhere closer to Big Lake came the throaty cry of a large cat. Ty didn't know about anyone else, but he thought one encounter with the local wildlife was enough for one day. He took the reins from the boy and signaled Ranger to a stop.

"We can do this again tomorrow if you want to," he suggested. At Jimmy's enthusiastic nod, he left the child in the saddle and dismounted. Before the kid got any ideas about taking an unauthorized solo ride, Ty lifted him and placed him safely on the ground. Expecting Sarah to rush over, gushing about how good Jimmy had looked on Ranger and asking a million questions, Ty scanned the surrounding area.

The social worker wasn't standing by the fence rail waiting for them. In fact, she was too busy talking with Matt Henson and John Padgett to even notice they'd finished their ride. Something twisted low in Ty's gut and his mouth pulled to one side.

"C'mon, kiddo," he said, clasping a hand on Jimmy's shoulder. "Let's go see what Ms. Sarah's up to. And then, I think I'll rustle up another slice of that apple pie."

"So, if I'm hearing you right, I should plan on two years before I see a dime of profit, and probably five until I earn enough to pay myself a decent salary."

To a man, the group standing in the circle nodded.

"That's about right," offered Matt. He scratched absentmindedly at a two-day growth of beard. "Over half of new businesses fail, mostly because the owners don't have a financial cushion to see them through those first crucial years."

"And a plant nursery?" Skepticism filled Elliott's eyes. "Things beyond your control could put you out of business before you even get off the ground. If you were bringing a new invention to market, you'd face a host of problems. But with tropical flowers, you'll have all those and more. Insects, drought, a cold snap…"

Elliott's words were so chilling Sarah shivered and buried her hands in the pockets of her sweatshirt. She hadn't intended to seek advice from the investment brokers. What had started out as a way to avoid watching Ty give Jimmy his first riding lesson had turned into a crash course in business finance. The guys had proven distracting, all right.

Just not like she'd hoped.

From the way Matt and his friends put it, her plan to turn her passion for gardening into a business that would produce enough income to let her quit her job at DCF simply wouldn't fly. She wouldn't be able to support herself, much less take in one or two foster kids.

Oh, she had savings. Enough to see her through if she walked away from her day job. But not enough for start-up costs and living expenses. At least, not five years' worth.

John Padgett broke in. "There is an alternative. You could invest. The market is turning around. I'm working with several companies that practically have a guaranteed—

"Uh-hum." Matt cleared his throat. "Save it for the office, John. We're not here to drum up new business."

Before Sarah could say she didn't mind, something slammed into the back of her legs. Her knees buckling, she stumbled forward a step. Several sets of hands reached to steady her. The others could have saved themselves the trouble. One strong arm wrapped around her waist and kept her upright.

"Watch out, boy. You almost knocked Ms. Sarah off her feet."

"Sorry, Ms. Sarah."

"Jimmy," she said, quickly stepping out of Ty's embrace. "It's okay."

"Did you see me, Ms. Sarah? Me and Ranger are pals. I steered him all by myself."

All too aware of the brooding male presence behind the little boy, Sarah fixed her focus on Jimmy's upturned face. "Ranger and *I* are pals."

Jimmy's cheeks scrunched. "Oh. Did you ride Ranger, too?"

"No, I meant… Well, yes, I…" Her thoughts created a log jam that her mouth couldn't get past.

Oblivious, Jimmy rushed on. "He's high off the ground, isn't he? I was afraid I'd fall, but Mr. Ty, he held me tight."

And, there it was again. At the little boy's words, the afternoon came rushing back. Miles and miles of beautiful scenery, hours on horseback, the phone call that nearly turned disastrous, the snake—she saw it all. Yet everything paled in comparison to the strength of Ty's arms around her, the press of his chest against her back, the outdoorsy scent he wore like a cologne.

Yep, there she was, right back in the one place she'd been trying to forget.

Sarah ignored the shiver that passed through her in order to focus on Jimmy. "I'm sure you did a terrific job. Did you thank Mr. Ty?" She took a breath and held it, hoping she could look the big rancher in the eye without doing something mortifyingly stupid—like throwing herself into his arms. She found his feet first, and let her gaze slowly climb the muscular body of the man who'd saved her life but destroyed her equilibrium. Finally reaching his face, she tightened her gaze at the strained expression that darkened his brown eyes. "Everything okay?"

"Sure." Ty gave an oddly endearing shrug. "Just wondering what was going on is all."

"The guys were giving me a little financial advice." She gestured to the group. "I appreciate it." Sarah raised her chin. "You've kept me from making what could have been a terrible mistake. It's clear that I need to give the whole nursery idea a lot more thought before I jump into it."

She turned to Jimmy. "I think it's about time you had a bath, mister." She pretended to sniff the air above the boy's head. "You smell like a horse."

"Me and Mr. Ty was gonna find us another slice of that apple pie." Jimmy frowned.

"Mr. Ty and I," Sarah corrected. "You already had two slices of the world's best pie with supper. Any more, and you'll get a stomach ache."

A yawn punctuated Jimmy's "But I'm not sleepy."

"Duly noted." Sarah took the little boy's hand in hers. "Now, let's go get you bathed and ready for bed."

Ty's fingers on her forearm stopped her as she passed him. "You'll come out to the campfire later?"

Though the question stirred the desire to do exactly that, Sarah shook her head. "It's been a long day and I still have progress reports to write. My boss will expect to read them the minute I get back. Besides, I came on this cattle drive to help look after Jimmy." She let the "not hang out with cowboys" go unsaid, but it didn't matter. Ty's hand dropped from her arm.

Sarah turned away so Ty couldn't see her wince. That last bit had been a little harsh considering he'd saved her life earlier. And just now, he'd given Jimmy the attention and encouragement the little boy deserved. But seeing the rancher in his element had shown her a side of Ty she hadn't expected. It left her feeling vulnerable, uneasy. She didn't trust herself to be around him and though walking away was the hardest thing to do, it was also the safest.

REFUSING TO STARE AFTER Sarah like some moonstruck calf, Ty resolutely turned his back while she and Jimmy made their exit. For the next few minutes, he listened to the financial planners give an account of their day. As Elliott boasted about rounding up the most cows and Matt tried to outdo his brother, Ty put in a word here or there, but after a few minutes he had to admit his heart wasn't in the conversation. No matter how bold the claims or how wild the tales, nothing compared to the memory of holding Sarah. His arms folded across his chest, he fought to get the attractive redhead out of his thoughts and failed.

There was never any shortage of mind-numbing work on the Circle P and, spotting Seth across the yard, he started for the cattle pens. He hoped the foreman's report on the roundup would give him something more to think about than the way Sarah had curled against his chest.

"By my count, we got fifty-five head in the pens," Seth said.

Ty removed his hat and ran a hand through his hair. "We're ahead of schedule."

It seemed he'd underestimated the enthusiasm of his guest wranglers. When he'd planned out the cattle drive, he'd allowed three full days to cull fifty cows from the larger herd. This new crop of riders had accomplished the task in less than half the time.

"Best send word to Doc Watson." Ty had asked the vet to come to the bunkhouse near Big Lake and inspect the cattle before they left their temporary camp for Kissimmee. "If he can handle the examinations and vaccinations tomorrow, we'll get on the trail a day earlier than we expected."

"Already sent one of the boys back to the main house with a message. Got any idea what we're gonna do with these folks in the meantime?" Seth's chin jutted toward the fire pit where Matt and his buddies were stacking kindling and logs. "They won't want to sit around camp all day."

"The Garrisons'll probably welcome the chance to head down to Big Lake. I've never seen anybody so crazy about birds, have you?" While Seth laughed, Ty paused for a moment. "Make sure to send one or two of the boys with them."

Seth's eyes narrowed suspiciously, but when Ty didn't volunteer any more information, the foreman didn't ask. "I'll send Randy," he said, suggesting the senior wrangler. "And the rest of our guests? Any ideas for them?"

Ty scanned the sky where stars twinkled against a

cloudless backdrop. "What do you think? A good day to go fishing?" They always brought a few rods along, just in case.

Seth nodded. "Weatherman says a cold front's moving in by the day after next. Fish should be bitin'."

"Okay then." A drop in temperature always made the fish hungrier. "You'll let Doris know so we can have a fish fry tomorrow?"

Seth smacked his lips. "Good eatin', that. Care for a friendly wager on who catches the first one?"

"You got somebody in mind?" The four businessmen seemed like the type who'd spend a week each summer fishing for marlin aboard a chartered boat. Bass and bluegill, catfish and tilapia probably wouldn't hold their interest long. That left Sarah and Jimmy as their only choices in a game where the stakes were high.

"My money's on the kid," said Seth.

Ty hiked one brow. "Not many lakes in New York City. I doubt the boy's ever held a fishing pole."

"I'm countin' on beginner's luck," Seth said with a smile.

That left Ty to back Sarah, and his thoughts wandered until he envisioned her in his arms again, this time as he showed her how to cast a fly rod. Deciding that the next day had definite possibilities, he shook hands with Seth to seal the bet.

Whistling, Ty headed for the bunkhouse where he stocked the fishing gear in a closet under the stairs. Within the hour he'd spread an assortment of flies and lures across the kitchen table and was happily rigging rods for the morning. While he loaded a new line on the last of the poles, he couldn't quite decide which he looked forward to the most—the chance to spend more time with Sarah or the grin Jimmy would have when the boy landed his first fish.

BUT AT BREAKFAST THE NEXT morning, Jimmy showed his sullen side.

"I don't want to stay with Ms. Doris." He pushed food around his plate without taking a bite. "I rode Ranger yesterday. I did real good. Kelly gets to ride by herself. Why can't I?"

Ty was on the verge of telling the child to mind his manners when Sarah waved him off. "You're too little to ride on a horse all by yourself. Mr. Ty can't hold you on his lap all day."

"No fair." Jimmy's little arms crossed firmly across his narrow chest. Using his feet, he pushed away from the table.

Ty took one look at the kid who was trying so hard to get his mad on, and swallowed a chuckle. He clamped one hand on the boy's shoulder. "You've got to work on not looking so cute when you're angry, pardner." He let sympathy for the child creep into his voice. "As it turns out, we're going to let the horses take a rest today while we do a little fishing."

Jimmy's posture stiffened and the little boy squinted up at him. "I don't want to."

Ty had been around the kid long enough to recognize his words as shorthand for *I've never done that before.* He stared at the little guy. Something tickled in the back of his throat and he swallowed, hard.

"Fishin's easy." Ty drew in a deep breath. "I'll teach you everything you need to know. You eat some breakfast now, before we head to the lake."

Across the table, concern bloomed in Sarah's eyes. "I thought you said we had to stay away from the water."

She turned to one side. Her hands hidden from Jimmy's sight, she made a gesture as familiar to every UF alumni as the school's orange and blue.

Recognizing the Gator Chomp, Ty tried to put her fears at ease. "Normally, that'd be true, but we won't actually get *in* the water. There's a dock not far from here. It'll be safe enough."

Aware that he couldn't very well take Jimmy on a fishing expedition without Sarah's buy-in, Ty searched her face. A slow breath he hadn't realized he'd been holding seeped across his lips when he saw the trust sparkling in her hazel eyes. He stared at the woman whose smile brightened the entire room. He shook his head, puzzled by an odd sensation that he was looking at his future. At her enthusiastic "Sounds like fun," he tried the image on for size.

The woman brought new meaning to the word *bossy*. She found him sadly lacking as father material. She worked at a demanding job a hundred miles away from the ranch that occupied all his time and effort.

And yet…

The idea didn't feel nearly as foreign as it had a week ago. He couldn't deny his attraction to her. Couldn't forget how she'd felt in his arms or how empty he'd felt when she left them. When she looked at him with trust sparkling in her eyes, he wanted to be a better man. A man who would live up to all her expectations and more.

He cleared his throat.

"Guess we'd best get ready, then, if we're gonna catch us some fish for supper."

"We're going to eat them?" Jimmy looked down at his stomach as if he envisioned a wriggling fish inside it.

Sarah's laughter spilled across the table. Ty felt his own eyes crinkle at the corners. He met her gaze. The unguarded look he found there shot warmth straight into his midsection.

"Not to worry, little man," he said, giving Jimmy's tummy a playful poke. "We'll clean 'em and fry 'em up real good first."

That seemed to put an end to the youngster's doubts, and an hour after the last of the breakfast dishes had been cleared, the crew was ready to hit the road. Ty loaded rods, reels and the picnic lunch Doris had packed. As he suspected they might, the businessmen split up, some choosing to stay at the camp to work with the vet, others riding off with the Garrisons.

Ty led his group through a patch of scorched trees on the way to Little Lake. There, spiders had been busy spinning webs that spanned the posts on either side of the wooden dock he'd replaced after last year's fire. Ty sent one of his ranch hands to clear off the deck with a broom, a job that had a dual purpose since the sweeper would also check the water to make sure nothing with large teeth lurked nearby.

"You got your choice of fly rods or poles. Lures or night crawlers," Ty offered the fishing party.

Jimmy's hand shot skyward. "I want nite-callers. What are they?"

Ty didn't bother to fight a smile. "Night crawlers are like worms. Fish love 'em."

Sarah chose a rod and reel combination. Grabbing a pair of clippers, she removed the hook and deftly tied on a shiny lure while Ty's idea of teaching the slender redhead how to fish faded. The woman clearly knew her way around a hook and line.

"Who's going to land the first monster?" she teased.

Ty gazed into Jimmy's small, excited face and knew he couldn't let the boy down, even if it cost him his bet with Seth.

"We will!" Ty and Jimmy shouted. They traded high fives.

"Get ready, fish, here I come." Sarah headed for the end of the pier where she tossed out her line.

Ty rigged Jimmy's pole with a bobber and a weight. "You want to bait the hook?" he asked. He held out a large pail filled with moist, black dirt.

Jimmy peered inside, uncertainty clouding his fine features. "I don't see any worms."

"They're in there," Ty assured him. "You just have to dig around a little bit for them."

There wasn't a boy alive who didn't like squishy, slimy things and Jimmy proved no exception. He dug in with both hands and pulled out a six-inch worm.

"Good job, pardner," Ty said encouragingly. "Now we put it on the hook." He took the boy's trophy and made quick work of the task. "Okay, let's go catch us a fish."

Ty picked out a likely spot about halfway down the dock. His hands around Jimmy's small ones, he demonstrated the best way to make an easy cast. Once the boy's bait landed in the water with a soft plop, he pointed to the red-and-white ball that floated on the surface.

"Now, watch that bobber. When it ducks under, that means a fish liked your bait and took himself a good bite. Then, you pull back like this." He gave the rod a gentle tug. "I'm going to stand behind you and keep one hand on the pole just in case you hook a giant of a fish who wants *you* for dinner."

Jimmy's laugh rang out across the calm water. Ty

joined in, but he'd been serious about holding on to the rod. Though once alligators had bordered on extinction, the big lizards had made such a phenomenal comeback they now inhabited every wet spot bigger than a mud puddle throughout the state. With kids, there was always the chance equipment would wind up in the bottom of the murky lake. That meant someone would have to wade in after it. Not wanting to add an impromptu alligator wrestling match to the day's agenda, Ty held on tight.

Wondering if Sarah was having any luck, he stole a look toward the end of the dock. Awareness stirred within him as he took in her trim form. Sun sparkled off the water, setting her hair ablaze. His glance caught the slim redhead just as she turned to make a fresh cast, and he dipped his hat in salute. Slowly, the smile he'd been hoping for spread across her face. The differences between the prim, uptight woman in her office and this more relaxed, approachable version were as unmistakable as they were surprising. But knowing it was the wrong time and the wrong place to ogle the woman, he let his gaze linger only long enough to see Sarah cast her line.

Just his luck, she cast like a pro.

He didn't have another second to think about it because, at that moment, Jimmy's bobber dunked beneath the glassy surface of the lake. The boy tugged on the pole, and the rod tip dipped.

"Fish on!" Ty shouted. He cupped his hands over the boy's and showed him how to reel in. The kid caught on quick. Soon, a good-sized bream flopped onto the dock.

Jimmy jumped up and down pumping his fist into the air while Ty made certain the boy's flopping fish didn't pitch itself back into the water. When Sarah joined them, Ty handed her his phone.

"We have to take pictures," he proclaimed.

He posed for several shots of the grinning kid holding his fish.

"As soon as we get back, I'll print them out for you," he offered when they finished.

Sarah tipped her head, the hint of a frown worrying her eyes. "And one for yourself. I'm sure you'll always treasure it."

Noting the tension that edged her voice, Ty shrugged. "Yeah, sure."

Immediately, he read disappointment in the subtle slump of Sarah's shoulders and knew he was somehow to blame. Had she expected him to hang Jimmy's photo on the wall at the Circle P? A look at her expectant expression told him that was exactly what she wanted. He resisted his first instinct and bit back a scoffing remark. He let his gaze drop to the child whose fine features reminded him so much of his ex-wife.

Ty stopped to rub a hand through his hair and gave the idea a chance to grow. Millie would always be a cord that tied him to Jimmy. Now that he'd had some time to get used to the idea, inviting the boy to spend a week or two on the Circle P each summer wasn't out of the question. That earned the boy a spot on the wall, didn't it? He gave the only answer available to him and nodded gruffly to Sarah.

"Yeah, I would like that picture," he said before he steered things in another direction.

"It's gonna be mighty slim pickin's at dinner tonight if we don't catch us a mess of fish. What do you say, slugger?" he asked, trying like heck not to let the boy's wide smile melt his heart. "Think you and I can out-fish Ms. Sarah here? How 'bout if the loser has to clean the fish?"

"All right!" Jimmy picked up his rod.

Ty extended his hand for the obligatory shake to seal the deal, only to see Sarah eye him warily.

"Sure you want to make that bet?" she asked.

Challenge danced in her hazel eyes and Ty felt his own narrow. "Have you been holding out on us?" he asked.

"Hmm, maybe a little," she said, a smile teasing the corners of her mouth. She pointed toward a post where a taut cord stretched down to the water.

Now that he'd stopped to listen, Ty heard fish thrashing at the end of the stringer. The noise told him that Sarah had gotten a head start on filling their ice chest.

"Shh," she whispered. She sneaked a glance at Jimmy. "Don't tell."

"Wouldn't dream of it," Ty answered as Sarah's fingers slipped into his. The woman was full of surprises and, marveling at her warmth, he held on to her hand a little longer than necessary. He wanted more, wanted to pull her close, but aware they weren't alone, he resisted the urge. He broke away and turned toward Jimmy. The little tyke was already digging around in the bait bucket for another night crawler.

"Better get your line wet," Ty called, knowing he'd be the one stuck with the messy job of cleaning their catch and not minding one bit.

Chapter Eight

The morning they were to break camp and start the trek to Kissimmee, Sarah eased open the bunkhouse door on a day so new the sun was only a promising glow on the horizon. Standing in the doorway, she drew in a deep breath. Icy cold knifed into her lungs. She coughed. Smoke plumed in the air around her. A chill seeped through her boots, her socks and into her feet. She squinted, drawing her arms tight to her chest. Above a thick mist, the tops of palm trees floated like pom-poms in the distance.

Awed by the sudden change in the weather, she shivered. Only yesterday afternoon, they'd eaten outside, feasting on fresh-caught fish, hush puppies and all the fixings spread on long tables beneath shade trees. She stomped her feet.

A cheery tune cut through the sound-dampening fog. Seconds later, a familiar shape rounded the corner of the bunkhouse. Despite the freezing temperatures, Sarah felt a warm spot open in her chest when she noticed Ty, saw his footsteps falter and heard the last of his whistled notes fade. He changed direction and, as he headed toward her, his bright smile cleared the early morning cobwebs from her mind.

"Mornin'," he called with a slight tug on the brim of his cowboy hat. "You're up early."

"Had to make sure Jimmy was warm enough."

A wide grin split the lower half of Ty's face. "That little scamp couldn't get enough to eat last night, could he?"

Sarah let her smile deepen. Last night, Ty had insisted on keeping Jimmy's fish separate from the others. "A boy deserves to eat his first catch," he'd said, dishing the special fillet onto the child's plate. The kid had wolfed it down, then helped himself to seconds and thirds.

"You were right about the sunshine and fresh air being good for him. He slept through the night without waking a single time." Sarah crossed her fingers, hoping she'd dealt with the last of the boy's nightmares. She stilled as Ty began a slow inspection that started at the top of her head and ended somewhere below her jawline.

A frown creased his forehead. "But you didn't? Bed uncomfortable?"

"No," she hurried to reassure him. "No, it's fine."

With a sly glance and a teasing lift of his eyebrows, Ty continued as though he hadn't heard her. "'Cause I can offer you another place to sleep if you'd like."

The implication started a slow burn that coiled upward from below Sarah's waist. Thrown off guard by her visceral reaction, she sucked in a deep breath of icy air. Despite her traitorous body, she did not want to share Ty's bed. Much. At least not until she got to know him better. She clasped her arms more tightly and gave herself stern orders to get the conversation back onto a nice, safe topic…like the weather.

"I slept fine," she insisted, praying her face hadn't

turned a flaming red. "It's just that once I woke up, I couldn't get back to sleep." She didn't mention the worry that had driven her out of the room as soon as she rolled over and felt the nip in the air. "Any idea how low the temperatures dropped?"

Half hoping Ty would refuse to let her get away with changing the subject, she watched him scuff a boot through the grass. He waited for it to spring upright before he answered. "Probably not below forty," he said. "I heard freeze warnings were up as far south as Fort Pierce. The orange groves around Ocala got hit real bad."

The answer doused the last flicker of heat in Sarah's midsection. She worried her bottom lip. Most of her plants would survive one night of record lows, providing the sitter had covered them with blankets and sheets. Beyond that…

"It'll be another long night for the orange growers," Ty said with a glance at the cloudless sky. "They'll be running the irrigation systems for all they're worth." During a hard freeze, grove owners sprayed the trees with water, hoping the ice would insulate the branches and minimize loss.

"Crap," Sarah muttered. She doubted the sitter could protect her delicate tropical plants two nights in a row. Not sure she wanted to hear the answer, she asked Ty how long the cold snap would last.

"A couple of days at the most." He shrugged. "But you don't have to worry. I have extra coats and jackets for everyone, including Jimmy. We'll bundle you up real good. Or, you don't *have* to ride today. You could stay here at the bunkhouse, catch up with us once things warm up a bit."

A shiver that had nothing to do with low temperatures flooded through Sarah. “No, I’m fine. Honestly. It’s just…”

Her voice trailed off. Talking about her hobby seemed like such a waste of time when she really wanted to take advantage of the chance to get to know Ty better.

“What?” he prompted.

Sarah sighed. “I collect tropical plants. I’m worried about them.” To lose all her stock now, especially since she wouldn’t be making a trip to Hawaii to buy new ones anytime soon, well, that would make it hard to recover.

Ty blew out a long breath. “So that’s what smelled so good in your office. Those flowers kind of reminded me of the Islands. What were they?”

“Plumeria,” she answered, surprised that he’d noticed—and remembered—the fragrance. The man was rapidly tearing down his rough-and-tumble image and replacing it with something more endearing. Despite his continued refusal to accept Jimmy as his son, he’d gone out of his way to make sure the boy enjoyed himself. He’d treated her with such kindness and concern that she was only just beginning to realize how hard it was to figure out Ty Parker. She smiled at him, determined to put her best effort into the task.

“They’re native to Hawaii, but they grow pretty well in Florida…as long as they don’t freeze. Or the bugs don’t get to them. Or, in some cases, there’s too much sun.”

“Sounds a lot like cattle ranching.” Ty straightened. “Well, I hope your plants are okay. It’d be a shame to lose something so pretty.” The knowing glance he sent her way said flowers weren’t the only pretty thing he’d hate to lose. He stamped his feet against the cold-hardened ground. "Some hot coffee sounds mighty good right now. How about we rustle up a cup?"

Sarah started, suddenly aware that while she'd yammered on about her problems, they'd been standing outside in the freezing cold.

But any hope of a quiet chat with Ty evaporated the minute they reached the main room. There, Matt, Elliott and the Garrisons waited patiently while Doris bustled about, setting steaming trays of food on the buffet line. Sarah ducked her head so Ty wouldn't see the disappointment she knew had slipped onto her face.

"Duty calls," he whispered while the others hailed him with greetings that sounded far too hearty for this early in the day. "Rain check?"

"Sure thing," she said, meeting his gaze and seeing her own regret mirrored in his eyes. "I probably need to get Jimmy up and moving anyway."

While Ty moved off to make the expected small talk with the others, she shoved aside her misgivings about the lost opportunity with a reminder that another week of the cattle drive remained. She'd have plenty more chances to spend quality time with the rancher, and she was determined to make the best of them, beginning with the campfire tonight.

Immediately after breakfast, Doris, with Jimmy securely strapped into the seat beside her, headed north. There'd be a hot meal waiting by the time the cattle drive reached the next campsite. No one else seemed in a hurry to brave the cold, and several hours passed before the last duffel bag was tossed into the back of a pickup truck. Once they finally mounted up, Sarah joined the Garrisons and the businessmen who spread out at the back of the drive where they were told to be on the lookout for strays.

By late morning, though she hadn't spotted a single loose cow, Sarah agreed that Ty had been right about one thing—temperatures had risen considerably thanks to a sky filled with bright sunshine. She pulled Belle aside, shucked the heavy sweatshirt she'd pulled on over long sleeves and whipped it into a tight roll. Twisting around to tie it behind her saddle, she spotted a pair of enormous brown eyes watching her from behind a thick clump of palmetto bushes.

"Hey," she said softly. "What are you doing back here?"

Sarah gathered her reins, prepared to work Belle around the stray. A move that, as it turned out, wasn't necessary.

"Good girl," Sarah encouraged when the cow stepped from behind the bushes. So fat it had developed a gentle hump over her front shoulders, the animal sported a sleek gray coat that stood out from the rest of Ty's brown cattle. She prodded Belle and her pretty prize to catch up with the others.

They still lagged the last of the stragglers by a good margin when Sarah spotted a horse and rider headed her way. The broad shoulders she'd rested her head against were unmistakable, and she felt the gentle stirring of attraction she'd come to expect whenever Ty was in the vicinity. Her pulse rose until she was struck by how much her feelings toward the tall rancher had changed in the short time she'd spent on the Circle P.

The day Ty had marched Chris and Tim into her office, she hadn't understood his attitude. But day by day, he had chipped away at her initial impressions. She hadn't pegged him for the kind of guy who would notice, much less care about, her flowers. And yet, he did. She'd watched his relationship with Jimmy blossom. Their growing closeness raised her hopes that, by the time the cattle drive ended, he'd acknowledge the boy as his own.

And where will that leave me?

Sarah flinched. Sure, she'd have a hard time parting with the child when the time came. But that didn't account for the ache that spread across her chest when she thought of never seeing Ty again. Seconds later, she acknowledged a painful truth. She wasn't sure she wanted a future without both of them—the rancher and the boy—in her life. She drew a deep breath, trying to find her balance and missing it entirely.

She was still pondering how to handle her newfound feelings for Ty when he reined his horse to her side. "Where'd you find that cow?"

She frowned. The hands that had once whisked her away from danger held Ranger's reins in a stiff grip. The lips she'd considered kissing were set in an angry sneer. She realized that she might have once more misjudged Ty.

Sarah pointed over her shoulder. "She stepped, pretty as you please, out from behind a bush."

Ty whipped his hat from his head and slapped it against his leg. "Damn. I guess Ol' Man Tompkins was right after all. His cows have found a way onto my property. Which means, mine have probably found a way onto his."

Beneath the broad-brimmed hat Ty had insisted she wear to keep the sun off her face, Sarah blinked in confusion. "And that's a problem?"

"I'll say. I'll have to have the men check every inch of fence line between our two ranches to make sure this never happens again."

Sarah gave her surroundings a good look. As far as

she could tell, there wasn't any difference between the grazing land and palmettos on either side of the tightly stretched barbed-wire fence.

"What's mine is mine and what's yours is yours?" she asked hesitantly.

"That's only part of it. Tompkins's cattle—" he pointed to the cow Sarah had found "—they're Brahmans. I raise Andalusians. Tompkins and I don't see eye-to-eye on the best breeds, but there's one thing we do agree on. Mixing Brahmans and Andalusians, well, that just isn't right."

Sarah raised an eyebrow. Okay, so hers had a hump and its horns twisted a little differently, but a cow was a cow, wasn't it? "Does it really make such a difference?"

For a second, a scathing look was Ty's only answer. Leather creaked. Sarah shifted uneasily. She waited while he uncoiled the rope tied to his saddle.

"There's good money in pure-bred cattle." Ty deftly threw a loop over the cow's wattled neck. "Think of those fancy dog shows. You have a champion black Lab and a champion chow. You mate them to dogs with the same pedigree, people pay big money for the whelps. But you let that black Lab mate with that chow, and you end up with a mutt that's good for nothin'."

"So a Brahman cow on your side of the fence, that's a bad thing." Sarah nodded. Now that he'd explained it, his reasoning made sense. "I guess I still have a lot to learn about ranching. In some ways, it's probably easier to deal with people. Don't get me started on their problems, but at least their pedigree doesn't matter."

Her comment generated a few alarm bells when Ty frowned. Hating herself for even asking, Sarah ventured the question she couldn't ignore. "Are you telling me that if Jimmy isn't your biological son…"

Exasperation showed in the firm line of lips she'd considered kissable.

"If he's not my blood, then I can't very well claim him as my son, can I?"

Ty clamped his hat onto his head. He tugged it until it shadowed his eyes.

"The trail follows the fence line. We'll probably spot Tompkins somewhere along the way," he said, his voice brusque. "We'll return his cow when we see him. For now, keep her away from the rest of my herd."

Sarah caught the end of the rope Ty flipped toward her without so much as a glance in her direction. And with that, he peeled off and started issuing orders to a couple of the hands, leaving her to stare after him.

How had she been so blind?

She'd assumed that once Ty got to know Jimmy well enough, once the little boy had wormed his way into the big rancher's heart, he wouldn't be able to part with the kid any more than she could. Now that she knew the truth, she felt a shiver of fear for the child's future.

TY SPENT THE NEXT HALF HOUR issuing tight-lipped orders that would guarantee every inch of the ranch's fence line was checked and double-checked before the herd pulled into Kissimmee. By the time he finished and had spoken with every rider and guest, the morning had evaporated much the same way as the fog that had rolled off the lakes the night before. He wished his anger had disappeared, as well, but there was no use denying he was on edge.

The reason trailed behind the rest of the herd.

As much as possible, Ty avoided looking over his shoulder at Sarah and the cow she'd so proudly corralled. Only a greenhorn could overlook the obvious.

The Brahman was nearly ready to calve. And that little fact was bound to cause another ripple in his already tense relations with Tompkins. The owner of the adjoining ranch had never ascribed to a live-and-let-live philosophy. Eager to expand his holdings, he'd seen his chance slip through his greedy fingers when Ty took over the Circle P. Therein lay the crux of a thorny problem. If things didn't go well with Tompkins, the man was apt to do something stupid. Knowing Sarah would be there to see it happen, Ty whispered a curse.

When Ranger's gait stiffened, he realized the horse had picked up on his emotions. He sucked in a deep breath and let it out slowly.

"Steady now," he said low and easy.

Despite his best efforts, his gaze strayed toward Sarah. An image of her riding alongside him across the wide-open ranchland took shape. He shook his head, trying to dislodge it. The woman was only visiting the Circle P. And that was a good thing. A very good thing. The curvy redhead had a soft spot for every cur that came her way. If she called the ranch home, they'd have a pack of mongrel dogs running around the place in no time.

Not that it was likely Sarah would abandon the city for life on a ranch. Other than their almost-kiss the day she'd run into the rattlesnake, she hadn't shown much interest in him. Yet, he couldn't deny he was attracted to the saucy social worker.

Up ahead, light glinted, harsh and bright off the hood of an ancient pickup truck, a sure sign Tompkins was in the vicinity. Though the outcome of talking to the man was apt to ruin what was left of his day, Ty signaled Sarah. He led the way to the property line where several downed fence posts trailed barbed wire loosely across the ground.

"Afternoon," Ty said, doffing his hat. "I see you're doing a little repair work."

Tompkins plunged a post-hole digger into the ground before he looked up. Rather than extracting the twin shovels of dirt, he leaned against the handle. "Looks like your blame fool cows knocked down a stretch of my fence again."

Ty gave the area in question a quick study. The posts and wire were a tangled mess, but they leaned away from Tompkins's property onto his. He folded his hands across his saddle's pommel.

"Looks to me like those posts were pushed over from your side. I'd be glad to have some of the men lend you a hand in making things right."

"Reckon I'm not too old to string fence." Tompkins rubbed a bandana beneath his sweat-stained hat. "Bit early for your summer roundup, isn't it? You sellin' off more of your herd to make ends meet?"

"Hate to disappoint you, but no." Ty grimaced. After his dad died, he'd come closer to having the ranch sold out from under him than he liked to admit. Turning the annual drive into a tourist attraction had saved him from bankruptcy. Now, more than a thousand Andalusians grazed on Circle P land and, if the Garrisons suggestion about birding tours held true, he was on his way to making some real money.

"So, you're on your way to Kissimmee?"

"Mr. Tompkins, this here's Sarah Magarity." Ty twitched a thumb in her direction. "She found one of your cows this morning. Thought we might as well deliver it to you as long as we were going past."

Ty rounded Sarah's horse and took the rope from

her. The old man's face clouded over when the cow, which had lagged several yards behind Belle, stepped into view.

"Shee-it." Tompkins spit and a dark brown stream hit the ground at his feet. "Let me get my 30-30." He spun toward a truck loaded with fence posts and bailing wire.

Ty's glance took in Sarah's puzzled look. She hadn't figured it out, but she would soon enough.

"You might want to head back to Seth and the rest of the crew," he said, trying to shield her.

"No, that's okay, I—"

Reality dawned in her pretty eyes, alarm darkening their depths when Tompkins reached into the gun rack mounted behind the driver's seat of his pickup. Carrying the rifle in the crook of one elbow, he retraced his steps.

Metal jangled. Belle's heavy hooves brought Sarah even with Ranger.

"He's not planning on doing what I think he is?" she asked, breathless.

"I'm afraid so."

Her eyes widened. "But why? Is there something wrong with the cow? Is she sick?"

"Not exactly." Ty gestured toward the Brahman's wide gray sides. "She's pregnant. Since she was found on Parker land, there's no tellin' whose bull did the deed."

Sarah's hands tightened into fists. She crossed her arms firmly below her ample chest. "You can't let him kill her."

Ty fought the urge to groan. Hadn't she been listening to a word he'd said earlier? Cattle weren't pets; they were livestock. "Purity of the bloodline is more important than the life of one cow. Tompkins can't have a half breed roaming around on his property any more than I can."

Tears filled Sarah's eyes. Seeing them twisted something in Ty's gut. He longed to put his arm around her, ease her pain, but what Tompkins did with his own property was up to him.

The older man slipped Ty's noose over the cow's head and handed the rope back to him with a "Much obliged" that was anything but. "Go on now, gal," he called.

The Brahman moseyed forward like she had all the time in the world, but when she reached the strands of new barbed wire stretched along the ground, she balked. Tompkins slapped her on the rump. "Git across now."

"Stop. I'll take her."

Ty swung toward Sarah. "Now, wait a minute," he began. His focus dropped to her quivering lower lip and he promptly lost track of whatever else he'd been about to say.

"I'll take her," Sarah repeated.

Tompkins whirled around, his gaze turning from surprised to crafty in less time than it took to swat a fly. "You want to buy her?"

"Sure," Sarah shrugged. "How much?"

"Fifteen hundred."

Ty cleared his throat. The cow was getting on in years. This would probably be her last calving season. He started to tell Sarah she was being played but saved his breath. She'd already figured that much out on her own.

"Ridiculous," she huffed. "You were just getting ready to put the cow down. You wouldn't have gotten a red cent for her if you had."

Tompkins's jaw came up. "Well, I might have been a bit hasty. I'd have come to my senses. Sold her for meat." He paused a long moment before adding, "Her and the calf."

Though the man was deliberately baiting Sarah, she rocked back in her saddle, looking for all the world like someone who bought and sold cattle every day of her life.

"How much," she demanded. She leaned forward, her eyes glowering, her face flushed. "And this time, give me a real price."

"Five hundred."

"I'll give you fifty," Sarah countered.

"You drive a hard bargain, missy," Tompkins said through a glimmer of a smile. "Okay, fifty for the cow. The calf, now that's another story. If it's a Brahman, I'm going to want it back."

For the first time since she'd made the ridiculous offer, Sarah turned to face him.

Staring at the pretty redhead, Ty gulped. The desire to give her whatever she wanted stirred within him. *No* dropped right out of his vocabulary.

"All right," he said. He swung back to eyeball Tompkins. "Long as you pay for the blood tests."

"Agreed," the old man said.

Ty managed not to groan as he looped the halter over the pregnant cow. Feed and veterinary bills for an animal that wasn't even his, one that was sure to cause more complications than he wanted to handle, would eat into his savings. He should be angry, he told himself. But the happy glow in Sarah's eyes was worth the cost.

Chapter Nine

"I'm going to call her Lacy," Jimmy announced. "'Cause her neck is all wiggly." He thrust a handful of grass through the slats of the pen Ty's staff had erected on the outskirts of camp.

"That's a good name," Sarah said, eyeing the ruffled folds of the cow's heavy dewlap. Her gaze swung to the boy who was intent on turning "Lacy" into a pet. "But you know we can't keep her," she cautioned.

"Why not?"

At the innocent question, her hand fisted. Slowly, she splayed her fingers. The pros and cons of letting the boy make friends with the rescued cow had played teeter-totter on her shoulders ever since they arrived at camp this evening. Another loss was the last thing Jimmy needed in his life. On the other hand, she didn't want the boy to wall himself off from new friends, new experiences.

"She's too big to sleep in your room," she teased.

Jimmy's forlorn look settled on the cow, which stood placidly chewing its cud on the far side of the pen. "She's lonely out here all by herself."

"Oh, I think she likes it. Some of the other cows can be pushy. They might not let her eat as much grass as she wants." Sarah gestured to the roomy area Ty had set aside for his latest acquisition after insisting the Brahman could not mingle with his recently inspected herd. "Here she has a whole pen just to herself. It's kind of like having your own bedroom."

"At my old house, we all lived in one room," Jimmy stated simply.

"Oh, yeah?" This was one of the first times the boy had opened up about his life in New York, and Sarah tried to picture the kind of place a struggling actress and waitress might be able to afford in a city known for its high cost of living. "Where did everybody sleep?"

"Miss Candy's bed was magic." Awe edged Jimmy's voice. "She made it disappear into the wall."

"She did?" A Murphy bed, Sarah thought. She'd never seen one, but it would be perfect for a tiny apartment.

"Not every day," he said, turning defensive. "But it did sometimes."

She hadn't meant to sound as if she doubted the boy and hurried to move the conversation forward. "And you? Did you have a magic bed, too?"

"No." Jimmy shook his head. "My mom and me slept in the corner. Our bed was on the floor. Her end was at the top. Mine was at the bottom. Sometimes it'd get cold and she'd let me sleep beside her." The little boy's hand dropped to his side. His fingers opened and the grass he'd been holding fell. He peered up, his eyes pinned on Sarah. "I miss my mom. She's been gone a long time. When's she coming home?"

Sarah slipped an arm around the boy's shoulders and hugged him close. "Oh, honey," she said softly. "I know she'd be with you if she could." His loss touched her heart, prompting a split-second decision to ignore

DCF's mandate against any talk of religion. "She's watching out for you from heaven."

Jimmy peered owlishly at the darkening sky where the first stars of the night twinkled. "How come I can't see her?"

"She's too far away, honey."

"I wish she was here with me."

The sad little-boy sigh tore another hole in Sarah's heart.

He thought for a moment. "Maybe I can go be with her there?"

Sarah blinked rapidly to keep her own tears at bay. "Not for a long, long time. But you can talk to her every night when you say your prayers." Jimmy had knelt on the floor and said his Now-I-lay-me-down-to-sleeps every night since Candy had dropped him off.

Jimmy silently considered this piece of information. "Okay," he said with a yawn.

She encouraged him to say good-night to Lacy. As he sprinkled a final handful of grass into the pen, the boy's head sagged. It was no wonder the little tyke was tired, Sarah thought. After a day on the trail, her own muscles cried out for a long soak in a hot tub. She settled for the feel of tiny fingers in hers as they walked back to the new campsite where, instead of one large bunkhouse, ten small cabins had been erected in a semicircle around an open fire pit.

By the time Jimmy said his prayers, he could barely keep his eyes open. He scrambled beneath the covers, and Sarah waited until his breathing grew even and his body stretched into a loose-limbed sprawl across the bed. Convinced he was down for the night, she drew in a steadying breath. Earlier today, she'd made herself a promise. And now, with the bonfire only steps away from their cabin, it was time to put her plan into action. Time to get to know Ty a little better.

She paused just long enough to gather her courage before she tugged on her jacket and drew a scarf around her neck. Though the day had warmed nicely, after sundown temperatures had plummeted again. Slipping through the door, she spotted Ty among the guests and staff who'd gathered around a roaring fire. Sparks danced in the smoke that rose between them, but a welcoming smile broke across his face when he saw her step into the circle around the bonfire.

"Jimmy down for the night?" Ty stopped strumming his guitar long enough to pat an empty spot beside him. "Sit here, why don't you?"

She glanced around at the others. Matt and Elliott and their pals huddled directly across the fire where they furtively passed a flask amongst them. Tom, Hope and Kelly had spread out on one side and were busy roasting marshmallows. Across from them, Seth and Doris did the same.

"Your turn to pick a song, Matt," Ty said while Sarah got settled.

"'Camptown Races,'" Matt replied quickly.

"'Camptown Races' it is." Ty's long fingers danced across the strings of a guitar that bore the scars of long use.

Sarah joined in singing the lively song, stretching her hands and feet toward the fire, very much aware of the man beside her. She hadn't inherited her sister's musical genius, but she had some idea of how long it took to master an instrument. How had Ty found the time? It was yet another facet of the man she wanted to get to know.

"Elliott, your turn," Ty said after the closing bars of Matt's selection faded.

And around the circle they went, each choosing familiar songs while, every so often, Seth interrupted to share a story or a joke. Eventually, Doris called it a night. One by one, the others left until only Sarah and Ty lingered by the fire while he sang a haunting ballad about lost loves and second chances.

Right then, right there, Sarah knew she was in big trouble. Contrary to the tales she'd been told by her foster kids, Ty Parker was a good man. An admirable man. A man she could trust. One who stirred a desire for the kind of life she hadn't thought possible before she met him. Now it turned out he was quite an accomplished guitarist. She held her hands to the crackling fire and forced herself to ask him a question.

"My brother picks a little. He's not nearly as good at it as you are. Have you been playing long?"

"All my life, or near about." Ty leaned the six-string against a log and stretched his long legs toward the fire. "I think I got my first guitar when I was about Jimmy's age. My mom played a mean fiddle and Dad, he was a fair hand on the banjo. Seth is, too. Some of my best memories are of us sitting around the living room after supper, playing and singing." His voice dropped an octave. "Good days, those."

He clasped his fingers in front of the fire. "You say you have a brother?"

Sarah nodded. "He's a physicist at Cornell. Does ground-breaking research on things I'll never understand. My sister is the real musical talent in our family. She teaches piano at Juilliard."

She felt Ty's dark eyes on her and looked up to meet his questioning gaze. "What?"

"For some reason, I thought you'd grown up in foster care."

"Me?" Sarah chortled. "What gave you that idea?" She stopped. "Oh, because I'm with DCF."

"Yeah, something like that."

Color flooded Ty's face. Certain the light from the fire was playing tricks on her eyes, Sarah shifted marginally closer to him.

"Actually, my childhood was pretty normal. I grew up about three hours from here, in Melbourne. My folks still live there. Dad's an engineer, and Mom's a schoolteacher. You're right about one thing, though. People don't go into social work without a pretty good reason. Meagan was mine."

While Ty leaned closer, Sarah told him how a chance encounter had changed her life. The day she'd walked into the Starbucks near her dorm and spotted Meagan Shay bussing tables, she almost hadn't recognized her long-lost friend. She'd assumed Meagan was, like herself, a college student, working part-time for spending money. After all, she'd taken first communion with the bright-eyed girl; their grandparents hailed from the same county in Ireland, and they'd been best friends… right up to the day Meagan and her younger brother, Tommy, had disappeared in the middle of the girls' first semester of junior high.

But Meagan's middle-class life had come to an abrupt halt not long after her mom died and her dad fell into the bottle. DCF had stepped in, separating the Shay children. The siblings had fallen out of touch. Meagan had no idea where her brother was and, worse, she didn't seem to care. Once she'd aged out of foster care, she'd left school and worked at a series of dead-end jobs that usually ended with her getting fired for being high.

Over the next few months, as Sarah tried to befriend her childhood playmate, she came to see how the years of moving from one foster home to another had marked Meagan far more than the tattoos and piercings that gave her a fearsome look. But when jewelry and electronics began disappearing from her dorm room, Sarah started asking hard questions about how two girls from similar backgrounds could turn out so different from one another. Eventually, she decided that her parents had been wrong when they'd preached that people could be anything they wanted. Realizing that environment played a crucial role in determining the lives people led, she vowed to do everything she could to make sure no other child endured what her friend had.

"So, I switched majors from education to sociology," Sarah said, summing up the story. "I stayed at UF until I got my master's." She shook her head. "I was sure I could change the system, make a difference. But..." She expelled a breath that was half shiver, half sigh. "It's impossible."

The temperature had dropped even further. More cold air swept in, stealing warmth from the dying fire. Ty shifted closer until his leg pressed against hers.

"If you don't think you're having an influence on these kids' lives, you're wrong. I've seen how you go to bat for them. They're lucky to have you on their side. Look at Jimmy."

Sarah couldn't help but frown. "That's exactly what I mean.... Look at Jimmy. Our foster homes are filled to capacity, so DCF policy requires that he go into The Glades. Even though you and I both know it's the absolute worst place for a young boy."

She retrieved a stick from the ground and used it to poke at the coals. "The same thing happens over and over. Every time I point it out or try to change things, I put my career on the line."

Suddenly aware of how cold she was everywhere except where Ty's leg touched hers, Sarah fought a chill. She scooted ever-so-slightly closer to the warmth that seemed to radiate from the big man. When he stretched one arm around her, it felt only natural to rest her head against his shoulder. "The last few months, it's gotten to where I don't think I can follow the rules and still live with myself."

Ty leaned toward her, tucking her deeper into his arms. "Have you thought about leaving?"

"Yeah," Sarah admitted. "That's part of what I need to do on this trip—determine my next step. What I'd really like to do is to make a true commitment to kids like Jimmy, give them a permanent home."

To his credit, Ty only hugged her closer. "You mean like adoption?"

"The older the child, the more difficult that becomes. So, no, probably not." She plucked a string from her scarf and let the wind blow it away. "But a kid Jimmy's age—he goes into the system and he'll probably live fifteen or twenty different places before he turns eighteen. That kind of instability makes it hard to do well in school, develop relationships, be prepared for life. I think, working with one or two kids at a time, I can change that. Give them the kind of stability they need in order to succeed."

"Sounds like a good plan," Ty said. "So, why don't you do it?"

Sarah tried to ignore the way Ty's breath whispered into her hair, the sense of strength that rose from him, the heat that radiated from him. The truth was, his presence made her wish they were doing more than having a conversation beside the roaring fire. She cleared her throat and tried to remember his question.

"The usual reason—money. I've always loved orchids and, when I visited Hawaii right after I got my BA, I fell in love with plumeria. I thought I might open a tropical nursery. Now it looks as though I'll have to go back to the drawing board, find a different idea."

"I'm sure you'll come up with something," Ty said softly.

There didn't seem to be much more to say, but still Sarah lingered, enjoying the sensation of Ty's arm around her, the press of his hip against hers. She was just beginning to think it might be time to untangle herself from his warm embrace and head for her cabin when his voice breathed through her hair again.

"So, you like flowers, do you? After today, I thought maybe you had a thing for cows."

Sarah squirmed around to face him. "I wanted to say thanks for that." When Ty ducked his head as if it was nothing, she hurried to correct him. "I know what an imposition it is for you to take in that cow. Jimmy's named her Lacy, by the way."

Sarah's gaze locked on the slow smile that spread across Ty's face.

"He named the cow? Anyone tell him you don't do that on a ranch?"

"Well, no…" Sarah began. Knowing she had to quit staring at Ty's perfect lips, she looked up. She thought her heart might stop when his smoldering eyes met hers. His dark look burned with the same need she felt.

Ty leaned down and brushed his lips against hers. Searing heat passed through her at his touch. Slowly, he kissed her again, this time lingering to plunder her mouth until her breath quickened and she silently cursed the layers of sweaters and coats between them. When he finally drew back, she felt dazed and confused and a little uncertain.

Ty's touch stirred feelings within her she hadn't felt in, well, forever. And there was a quality to his kisses that felt like coming home, at once comforting and exciting. But sitting by the fire in the middle of camp was not the place she wanted to be when or if she and Ty ever went beyond a few heated kisses.

Reluctantly, she made her excuses and headed back to her cabin afraid she'd never be as warm under the covers as she was in Ty's arms.

TY STEPPED FROM THE CORRAL where he'd left Ranger in Seth's capable hands. Noting a dark smear along one edge of the horizon, he scanned the sky above the flat prairie. As he studied the distant storm and the flashes of lightning that danced behind the clouds, an uneasy feeling tightened his stomach. His gaze drifted past ten tiny cabins, his guests' accommodations for the night.

After their fifth full day since leaving the main camp down by the lake, the cattle had bedded down without any problem. If he squinted just right, he could spot the half-dozen riders who would watch the herd in shifts until morning. Seth and the rest of the hands were seeing to the horses, making sure each one got a good rubdown. Over in the pole barn where Doris had dished out tacos and enchiladas for supper, the cook supervised her helpers in the prep work for tomorrow's breakfast. Not long ago, he'd spotted Sarah and Jimmy on their way to the bathhouse, their arms filled with towels and clothes.

Everything was exactly as it should be.

So, why did he feel as jumpy as a frog in a den of cottonmouths?

Seeing Sarah probably had something to do with it. The past four nights, they'd lingered at the campfire long after everyone else. At breakfast this morning, one look into her hazel eyes had stirred the urge to kiss her senseless. Or take her hand in his and disappear into the nearest hayloft. He wanted to taste her lips, explore her curves, to whisper sweet nothings in her ear and hear her moan his name. He hadn't felt such an overwhelming attraction to a woman since he and Millie had called it quits, and he wasn't quite sure what to do about it.

Probably nothing, since the one thing he knew for sure was that spending quality time with Sarah didn't fit his current agenda. With the cattle drive's reputation as a family-friendly event at stake, and the Circle P dependent on the successful delivery of fifty head to the buyer in Kissimmee, he couldn't risk getting involved with one of his guests. For the umpteenth time since breakfast, Ty told himself he should keep his distance from the redhead whose surprisingly curvy body got his motor running.

A slow roll of thunder caught his attention, and he studied the sky again. Clouds that had hugged the horizon the last time he checked had moved a lot closer in the fifteen minutes he'd spent woolgathering. Ty rubbed the bridge of his nose. With no internet or cell phone coverage, he had to rely on his gut…and his gut told him they were in for a blow.

Immediately, he scrapped plans for the nightly bonfire. Though he might not mind a little weather if it gave him an excuse to hold Sarah in his arms, he didn't think the rest of the guests would feel the same way about hunkering down in the pouring rain. Instead, they'd have an old-fashioned hoedown. He'd gather everyone in the pole barn where he'd play the guitar, and Seth could join in on the banjo. Between them, they could manage some dance music. It wouldn't be the kind of show the city slickers were used to, but that was the whole point, wasn't it?

He'd started spreading the word for everyone to gather in the barn when he spotted Sarah headed his way. Though the sight of her ignited a warm glow in the center of his chest, he frowned when he didn't see Jimmy. She usually watched the boy like a mother hawk.

"Hey." He touched his hat brim and was rewarded with a smile bright enough to chase away the storm clouds…or at least make him forget about them for a moment. "Jimmy around?" More for his own benefit than Sarah's, he added, "Thought I'd see about his boots."

Earlier today, the kid had doused himself good when he kicked at a fresh cow pie. A shower and a change of clothes would put the boy to rights, but Ty thought he might show Jimmy the best way to clean his boots, the same way his father had shown him.

Sarah's pleased look changed into one of pure consternation. "He ran out fifteen minutes ago saying he had to talk to you about Lacy. You haven't seen him?"

"Nope." Ty watched aggravation turn to concern in Sarah's eyes, and knew exactly how she felt. After all, it hadn't been that long ago that he'd been the one to let the boy get out of his sight.

Ty shook his head. He'd deny it if anyone asked, but deep inside he knew that once they had the results of the blood tests and Sarah found Jimmy's real dad, he'd miss the kid. Sometimes, when he stopped to think about the boy riding on another man's shoulders or striving to match his strides as they crossed the room, an ache clawed at the back of his throat. At first, a reminder that the child wasn't his had been enough to let him shake it off. Lately, though, the feeling had lingered despite his best efforts to rid himself of it.

Distant thunder rolled ominously, and he glanced at the swiftly moving clouds that filled a third of the sky. The storm boiled toward them. From the field where they'd bedded down, the lowing of the cattle picked up its tempo, a sure sign that the herd was getting restless.

"Not to worry," Ty said, though worry was exactly what he felt. "We'll find him. I'll head back to the corral, check with Seth. You start with the cabins at the other end of the camp. He can't have gone far. Meet me back here in five minutes."

Hiding his concern for the boy's safety, Ty spun and jogged back the way he'd come. The truth was, the little tyke could be just about anywhere. He hated to think of what might happen if Jimmy had decided to strike out on his own with a storm nearing. He quickened his pace.

"Hey, Jimmy, you in here?" Ty called at the entrance to the barn. A quick search of the corral had yielded no sign of little boys or ranch foremen.

Seth poked his head out of a large storage locker. He held up a yellow slicker. "I was just about to hand out the rain gear."

Judging by the way angry clouds were rapidly blocking out the first stars of evening, Ty thought better of the idea. "Nah, don't do that. Call the men in." In a state where more people died of lightning strikes than anywhere else in the U.S., he wanted his men off the open field. "They can grab some coffee till the storm passes."

"And if the cattle spook?"

"Let 'em." Though a stampede was nothing to laugh at, the cows would stop when they reached the next watering hole or creek. "Not like there's a cliff or anything they can run themselves off of." He paused. "You seen Jimmy?"

Worry flickered in Seth's watery blue eyes. "Not a hide nor hair. Not since supper. Has the boy gone missing?"

"He told Sarah he was coming to see me, but he never made it. How 'bout helping us look for him?"

"You got it." Seth dumped the armload of rain gear on the floor and strode out of the barn as fast as his bowed legs would take him.

Ty began working his way back toward the center of camp. His pulse thumped harder every time he looked around a corner and didn't spot the child. He met up with Sarah, who'd run into Doris somewhere along the way. The cook raised her hands, palms up. Her calm demeanor didn't fool him for a minute. Though she and Seth had raised plenty of kids—including him and J.D.—Doris had also made enough trips to the E.R. to pay for a new wing at the hospital. She knew all too well the dangers a young boy could find.

He shifted his gaze to Sarah. Her voice climbing, she asked, "He wouldn't have gone to see Lacy on his own, would he?"

Ty swallowed a groan. The old branding pen where he'd put the cow for the night was a fair walk straight into the approaching storm.

"Guess I'd better check it out."

"I'm coming with you," Sarah insisted.

Ty started to argue, but one look at the sky convinced him there wasn't time for a discussion. "Let's hustle," he said simply.

They took off at a fast jog. Halfway to the stream that ran past the pen, Ty questioned the wisdom of the last two enchiladas he'd eaten at dinner. But the burning in his chest was more than indigestion. Concern for the child twisted his stomach into knots and made it practically impossible to draw a full breath. His feet plunged into the rapidly rising creek and the possibility of a future without the little tyke hit home. His chest seized. He didn't know what he'd do if anything happened to the child.

"I don't remember the water being this high," Sarah called over a gust of wind.

"Must be a hard rain upstream." A rain that would be on top of them within the hour. More for the chance to hold her than because she needed help, Ty grabbed Sarah's hand as they sloshed through water that had risen to their knees. He pointed. "The pen is just over that rise, there."

Bleached-white seashells crunching beneath their feet, they clambered over a low mound that had once been a landfill of sorts for an ancient Indian tribe. Ty stepped in front of Sarah as a palmetto branch churned past turning end-over-end like a tumbleweed. Relief surged through him the moment he spied Jimmy standing beside the slat-sided fence. In his pajamas and boots, the boy was such a comical sight, Ty didn't know whether to hug the child to death or yell at him for leaving the camp alone.

"Mr. Ty. Ms. Sarah. Did you come to see Lacy, too?" He smiled up at them.

Sarah started for the boy, but Ty was faster. He

scooped Jimmy up and hugged him tight to his chest. Recriminations could wait until later. For now, they had to get into the barn before the storm hit.

Or before they got run over by a herd of frightened cattle, he thought as a low drone filled the air.

Sarah heard it, too, and aimed a questioning look his way. If worry had filled her eyes before, something close to panic had risen in them now. "Is that rain?" she asked, hopefully.

Ty gave his head an abrupt shake. "Cattle. We need to get across the creek, now." He leaned forward, looking Jimmy square in the face. "Hey, kiddo. I'm going to swing you around onto my back. You hang on good and tight 'cause we're gonna run."

Sarah's hand in his, Jimmy hanging on for dear life, back to the stream they ran while the drone turned into the sound of thundering hooves and bellowing cattle. Ty's feet hit the far bank where he risked a quick look over one shoulder just as the first wide-eyed cow crested the small rise behind them. With Sarah's and Jimmy's lives in his hands, he prayed that the cows would stop when they reached the water's edge.

Just in case they didn't, he aimed for a small copse of scrub oak. The trees weren't tall and they wouldn't offer much protection if the herd headed their way, but it was the best he could do under the circumstances. Outrunning a stampede was not an option.

He boosted Jimmy into the highest branches and ordered the child to stay put. His arms around Sarah's waist, he helped her scramble onto a nearby limb.

"What about you?" she asked.

"Don't you worry about me. They won't come this far." At least, he hoped they wouldn't. If they did, he'd do his best to turn them aside and protect the ones he cared for.

Ty drew in a deep breath as the first of the milling throng of cattle took one look at the creek and veered north. Fifty head of cattle weren't enough to make the ground shake, but Ty thought it sure felt like it when the bellowing herd thundered past.

"Where'd they go?" Jimmy wanted to know when the last cow had disappeared.

"Not far," Ty answered. "They'll run for a while, till they figure out they can't outrun the storm. Then, they'll settle down." There hadn't been time to worry if nearly being trampled to death would scar Jimmy for life. Now that the danger had passed, he searched the boy's face and breathed a sigh of relief at the awed excitement he saw there.

As if to remind him why he'd come looking for Jimmy in the first place, another crack of lightning lit the darkening sky. Ty automatically counted the seconds. He reached fourteen before the thunder rolled.

Damn. The storm was less than two miles out and moving closer by the second.

"We don't want to be in these trees anymore. Time to make tracks."

He nodded to Sarah, swung Jimmy onto his shoulders and off they ran. Dodging palm fronds that sailed past in the freshening breeze, they covered the ground quickly. Still, rain pelted them before they were halfway back to the campsite. They ducked into the barn seconds before thunder clapped on the heels of a nearby lightning strike.

Ty grasped Sarah's hand and pulled her close while he held Jimmy in a tight embrace. He wondered if this was what it was meant to be a husband, a father—to protect the ones you love. If it was, he thought, it was exactly what he wanted.

A not-so-discreet throat clearing brought awareness that they had an audience. Ty gave Sarah a final squeeze and gently kissed the top of Jimmy's head before he set the little tyke on the ground. While Doris rushed over with towels and Jimmy regaled her with the story of his exciting adventure, Ty stood, his arms folded across his chest.

Okay, so the boy probably wasn't his. But the experience they'd shared had put things in a new perspective. Millie had been his wife and, by law, he was the child's father. He wanted to be there for all the important events in Jimmy's life, to keep him safe, and to help the boy become a man. Knowing what a huge task he was about to undertake, he sought Sarah's gaze. Once he told her what he planned to do, would she walk away, her job complete? Or could he make her stay?

Chapter Ten

Sarah thought her jaw might hang open when Ty simply shrugged aside a few congratulatory slaps on the back and went to look for his guitar. Or at least she did until she looked into Ty's dark eyes and saw that he was putting on a brave front. For Jimmy's sake. For all their sakes. In that moment, she admitted to herself she'd fallen the tiniest bit in love.

Forcing herself to follow Ty's example, she squared her shoulders and straightened her trembling lips into a bright smile. When some of the ranch hands staged an impromptu flat-foot competition, she led Jimmy into the circle. Feet slapped faster and faster against the plywood floor in a hybrid mix of Irish folk and tap dance. Soon the little boy's laughter competed with Ty's guitar, Seth's banjo and the welcome thunder of clapping hands. By the time Josh walked off with a dish of Doris's peach cobbler, his prize for the best performance, Sarah had developed a strong case of hero worship to go along with her deepening feelings for the man who'd saved her life.

Unwilling to leave his side once the storm abated and the party broke up, she watched Ty saddle Ranger.

"You're going out?" she asked, amazed that he was still able to function after all they'd been through.

"Told the men I'd take first watch with the herd." Ty lifted the stirrup over Ranger's back and pulled the cinch to tighten it.

"Can I come?" she asked before she could stop herself. She held her breath wondering what she'd do if he didn't want her company. If, despite not saying a word about it, he was angry with her for letting Jimmy slip away from camp.

Ty tilted his head to give her an inquiring look. In a voice that bore no trace of reproach, he asked, "What about Jimmy?"

"Doris and Seth asked him to spend the night in their cabin." She scuffed one foot against the rain-soaked ground, surprised by a sudden onset of shyness. "I think she blames me for putting us all in danger."

"Don't even go there." Ty guided the stirrup into place and turned to face her. "Doris is just smitten with young James. We all are. Besides, if I recall correctly, you weren't the first to let that boy get out of sight."

His soothing tone put an end to the accusations she'd been hurling at herself ever since she'd realized Jimmy was missing. She let out a deep breath and blinked back tears.

Ty placed one finger beneath her chin and lifted until she met his gaze. "I'd love to have the company if you aren't too tired."

As keyed up as she felt after their brush with death, sleep was hours away. Gazing at the man who was dangerously close to stealing her heart, she wondered what it'd be like to spend the rest of her life with someone who doled out forgiveness like a second helping of dessert. She swallowed. "Give me a minute to saddle Belle, and I'll join you."

Moments later, they led the horses into a night which, like the storm, had worn itself out. Away from the lights of the city, a million stars glinted against a pitch-black sky. Damp grass muted the sounds of the horses hooves enough that Sarah heard water babbling in the creek. In the distance an owl hooted.

"That was one of the tightest spots I've ever been in," she admitted when Ty pulled Ranger to a halt upwind of the exhausted cattle. A shiver passed through her as she wondered what might have happened if he hadn't been there.

"Everything turned out okay. As long as you and Jimmy didn't get hurt, there's nothing to worry about."

The last wispy cloud sailed away from the moon, and silver light bathed the open field, but Sarah didn't have to see the rancher to know his aw-shucks-ma'am grin was firmly in place. "We're fine, thanks to you," she whispered.

Six months ago, she'd been too intent on protecting her charges to listen to Ty's side of the story. Now, she needed to know every detail about the failed Big Brother program. "You were so calm, so wonderful with Jimmy, it made me realize that Chris and Tim had to have been perfect hellions to get under your skin the way they did. What did they do that was bad enough to get them sent home?"

For a long minute, Ty didn't answer and Sarah thought she'd hit a nerve. Her breath stalled, not starting again until he lifted his hat and brushed a hand through his hair.

"They acted as if the rules were meant for everyone but them. I held my tongue and didn't say anything until one of ‘em snuck out for a smoke. Fool kid started a grass fire.”

“Fire?” Sarah sucked in a sharp breath. She remembered the blackened trees and scorched earth around Little Lake. No wonder Ty had been so upset with the boys.

“It was just pure luck we were close to water. We only lost a few acres, and the grass there’ll grow back eventually. It could have been a lot worse.”

“Ty, I’m so sorry,” Sarah said, shaking her head.

“If they’d said so much as one word about being sorry for what they’d done, I’d have kept ’em on for the rest of the drive. But they copped an attitude, and I couldn’t risk ’em pulling some other fool stunt.”

Which explained why he’d shown up in her office full of piss and vinegar, but not why he’d had sole responsibility for the boys. Hadn’t the Big Brother program been a fraternity project?

“It never seemed fair that your friends put up the money for the program, but you got stuck doing all the work,” she offered.

“I wanted it that way. As a tribute to J.D.”

“Your friend? I saw his picture that first day at the Circle P. Doris said you two were close.”

“Yeah.” Ty snorted. “You could say that. Two peas in a pod, she called us. From the day we met, all the way through high school, we did practically everything together. Baseball. Horseback riding. Fishing. Summers, weeks would pass when we never even left the Circle P.”

Having spent the past six days on a cattle drive through some of the prettiest country she’d ever seen, Sarah understood the attraction. But the social worker in her wondered at a different aspect of the story. She lifted one eyebrow. "His parents didn't mind?"

"Only when they sobered up long enough to notice he was missing. Which wasn't often. His folks weren't worth a nickel, but J.D., he was the brother I never had. Always the peacekeeper." He chuckled. "With Seth and Doris's brood on the ranch back then, by the end of the day, we usually needed one."

"Sounds like he was an exceptional friend."

"Yeah," he said tightly. "Even after Millie and I got serious, it was always the three of us. She'd cheer at our football games on Friday nights. We'd take her to the movies on Saturdays."

Ty slapped his hat against his knee.

"J.D. was right about one thing—he said all along that Millie wasn't right for me, wasn't the kind of gal who'd stick around. Even when moving back to the ranch was the farthest thing from my mind, he insisted I could do better."

"But you married her anyway."

Leather creaked as Ty squared himself in Ranger's saddle. "She was my first. First love, that is. All through high school, she led me around the way teenage girls lead randy teenage boys. When I left for college, I thought she was worth waiting for."

While Ty filled her in on his history with Millie, Sarah fought a growing dislike for Jimmy's mom. From the story he told, it sounded as if the rancher had done everything he could to earn his wife's love, when love should be something freely given and not paid for with fancy houses in the city.

"I'm making her sound like a bad person, and she wasn't," he said at last. "Maybe she was the right person at the wrong time. Or maybe our marriage was doomed no matter what we did. Who knows? I do know I was already restless by the time my dad got sick. Tired of suits and ties and long commutes. For me, coming back to the ranch was the best decision I'd ever made. But Millie, she never accepted my struggle to keep a roof over our heads, the land beneath our feet."

Sarah swept their surroundings with an encompassing gesture. Even in the dark, the beauty of the land was unmistakable. "I'm not sure how anyone could turn their back on all this."

"There was a time I didn't think I'd ever set foot on the Circle P again so, to a certain extent, I can understand the way Millie felt. The other stuff was harder to see past."

Ranger snorted and pawed the ground with one hoof. Ty took a moment to calm the horse, and when he continued his own agitation had faded, making him sound more sure of himself.

"I got through J.D.'s funeral on my own. Not telling me about the baby, that's a little harder to understand. Since she's not here to ask, I guess there's some questions I'll carry to my grave."

Sarah let a sigh ease out between her lips. She had her own unanswerable questions. Like why parents hurt their own children. How the very people who were supposed to provide a safe haven for victims of abuse and neglect often ended up causing more harm than good. How she could continue to work for a system that was so hopelessly broken. "Some questions just don't have good answers," she murmured.

"And some do," came Ty's quiet response. The metal on Ranger's bridle jangled. "What do you think? Any room in your life for a rancher who's barely making ends meet?"

Across the open field, a restless whip-poor-will trilled notes into the dark.

"There might be," Sarah said past the lump in her throat. Belle's ears rose and she blew out a rough breath. "Easy girl," Sarah soothed. She rubbed one hand over the silky mane.

"I'd sure like it if you came back to the Circle P for a while after we deliver the cattle to Kissimmee."

Ty's voice had dropped so low Sarah had to lean in to hear him. Her answer, though, required no thought. It rose unbidden to her lips. "I'd like that," she said. "Very much."

THERE WAS NO SHORTAGE of unattached women within striking distance of the Circle P. And while he might never be voted the Most Eligible Bachelor in the state, Ty also understood the way things worked. One subtle hint that he was ready to dip his toe into the dating pool again, and the line of single women bearing casseroles and offering—well, whatever—would have stretched from the front gate to the highway. For that reason, among others, he'd played his cards close to his vest after his marriage crashed and burned. Six years later, it was a habit he found difficult to break. So the *Yee haw!* that bubbled up from his chest when Sarah agreed to visit the ranch came as a shock. He managed—barely—to clamp his mouth shut with a simple reminder that an unexpected noise could spook the cattle.

He wished he could control his heart as easily. It hammered so fiercely he was afraid Sarah could hear it from her seat on Belle's broad back. When his companion didn't aim an incredulous look his way, he thanked his lucky stars for the noise of chirping crickets, the faint scurry of opossum and armadillos that drowned out everything else.

Maybe he should have been a tad more specific when he'd asked Sarah to visit the Circle P. He wasn't ready to jump into a committed relationship. From here on out, he vowed to keep the conversation light and friendly and make damn sure he didn't imply his invitation was anything more than it was…a simple gesture, the chance to get to know each other better. In ways they couldn't explore while on a cattle drive where the staff and guests were aware of their every move.

He opened his mouth to clarify his intentions, but what came out was, "I've been thinking about your business idea."

Sarah's head whipped toward him. "You have?"

"Yeah."

He had? Sure he had. He just hadn't intended to mention it. At least, not yet. Maybe never. But now that he'd put his feelings on the table, his mouth seemed to have developed a mind of its own.

"Establishing a plant nursery in Fort Pierce is an expensive proposition. Land prices are against you from the get-go."

"To say nothing of the occasional freeze," Sarah murmured.

"Yeah, there's that, too." Unable to help himself, he swept his hand through the air. "I have a thousand acres on the Circle P. There's even an old greenhouse out behind the main house. No one's used it in years, but I'm sure it wouldn't take much more than a fair amount of elbow grease to set it to rights."

A distant *mrrruuh* from one of the cattle broke the stillness of the night. Ty waited, intently aware that Sarah had shifted around in her saddle to face him. Had he said too much? Tried too hard? He held his breath, silently cursing his runaway mouth.

Sarah's head tilted until one of her braids brushed her shirt just above the pocket. "Are you…are you suggesting I open a business *here?*"

"Not right away, of course," he said, finally regaining enough of his senses to do some much needed backpedaling. "But it might solve some of your problems. Eventually."

Shut up, he told himself. Shut up. Shut up. But the dam had been breached and now that the floodgates were open, he couldn't stop.

"What do you think?"

"Why would I do that, Ty?"

Sarah might be the girl of his dreams, but she was no pushover. She'd always demand more than he intended to give. Push him to be a better man than he might have been otherwise. It was one of the things he liked most about her…when it didn't drive him crazy like it was doing right now.

Trying to sound more self-assured and confident than he felt, Ty said, "For one thing, the Circle P's below the frost line."

"No other reason?"

She'd called his bluff. There was no way around it. He had to lay his final card on the table. "Well, there's me." He wanted, needed, to know if there was a future for them. "So, what do you think?"

"How about we take it one step at a time and see where the road leads."

"Sounds like a plan," he agreed. Especially if that road led where he hoped it would.

He settled into the saddle, the pounding of his heart easing. Comfortable with the decision they'd made, he spent the next few minutes dreaming of what the future might hold for them. The idea of coming home to a house filled with love and laughter instead of silence and empty rooms deepened the smile on his lips. He pictured Sarah standing on the wide front porch, a baby in her arms and Jimmy at her side. The image gave way to one of a little girl with Sarah's red hair and his brown eyes playing hide-and-seek with her big brother in the barn. He frowned at the pitchfork a careless hand had left propped in a corner, and snapped to attention, determined to read someone the riot act.

Had he been dreaming?

Ty blinked. He glanced to his side where Sarah had fallen quiet. Had she drifted off, too? Her eyes wide-open, she stared at distant trees. Apparently, he'd given them both a lot to consider. In two days, they'd make Kissimmee, and the group would head home to their own beds. He shook his head, trying to dispel the image of Sarah in his.

From somewhere nearby, a horse nickered. When Ranger whinnied in response, Ty pulled himself straighter in the saddle. In the light of the half moon, he spotted two riders slowly moving toward them.

"Ms. Sarah. Boss." The words floated out of the dark. A silhouette on horseback tipped his hat. "How's it going?"

"All quiet out here, Randy," Ty said just loud enough to make himself heard.

"How can you call this quiet?" Swatting at something near his face, Josh rode alongside the lead wrangler. "That rain got everything stirred up, even the mosquitoes."

Ty canted his head to one side. From a long way off, the deep-throated roar of a bull alligator rose above a croaking chorus of frogs. It had been a long day, one filled with more unexpected twists and turns than a creek bed. He clucked to Ranger and said good-night to the men who'd watch over the herd until morning. And with Sarah at his side, he led the way back to the camp.

Once the horses were bedded down, he walked Sarah to her door. Would she invite him in? Though the idea was enough to wake him up a bit, Ty quickly discarded it. He'd made himself a promise not to get too involved while they were on the cattle drive. It was a promise he intended to keep. No matter how deeply in love he'd fallen.

He stumbled, barely avoiding a fall that would put him face-first in the dirt.

"Are you okay?" Sarah asked, her hand on his forearm.

"Yeah. Must 'a tripped over a rock or something," Ty said, though he knew full well the ground was level.

In love?

Was he in love? Cautiously, he tried the description on for size and was surprised at how well it fit. He was in love with Sarah Magarity. He probably had been since the moment he first saw her, that day in her office nearly a year ago. He'd known then there was something special about the redhead with the sparkling eyes, pert nose and kissable lips. When she'd turned on him after the episode with Chris and Tim, he'd admired her spunk, her willingness to go to bat for those entrusted to her care.

She could be stubborn. No doubt about it. He only had to look as far as Jimmy to know how stubborn. But he had to admire someone who stuck to her guns no matter what. The courage she'd shown during the stampede only added to her allure.

Ty ran a hand through his hair, amazed that he hadn't put two and two together before now. Here he'd thought they were just getting to know one another better these past few days, when, really, he was falling for the girl.

The idea was thrilling but a little scary.

At the door to her cabin, he braced one arm over her head.

"I'm going to kiss you now," he said, leaning down to brush her lips.

She met him halfway, her response stirring his desire. All hope of keeping things light and teasing disappeared in a red-hot flash. He swept into her mouth, at once possessing and plundering. She moaned softly, and he pressed against her, yearning to hold her, to touch her, to make her his own.

He was barely aware of her fingers tugging his shirt from his waistband. But when she caressed the sensitive skin at his waist, he stilled for a moment before slipping his own hand beneath the hem of her shirt. Of their own volition, his fingers traced the outline of her ribs, climbing, one step at a time slowly upward. By the time he reached the full curve of her breast, her breathing was fast and shallow. So was his. He heard a groan and wasn't sure which one of them made it.

He wanted nothing more than to take her breasts into his hands, his mouth, and lavish them with the kind of attention that would drive them both wild. But a rickety cot in a bare cabin wasn't the place he wanted to take Sarah to bed. At least, not the first time. Though it took every ounce of control he had, he eased his fingers away from their prize and slowly retraced his steps.

With one final taste of her lips, he drew her into his

arms, cradling her head below his shoulder. "No second thoughts about coming back to the Circle P with me?"

Sarah stirred in his arms. Her head tilted toward his. "Maybe one. You've seen him. Five years old? Cute as a button?"

"Jimmy. He'll come, too, of course." He nodded. He was the boy's legal parent. It was a responsibility he was ready to shoulder, one he wanted to share with Sarah.

He bent to tell her he'd had a change of heart about the boy. But her half-closed eyes stopped him. As much as he wanted to convince himself her lids were heavy with desire, he had to admit the truth—the long day had taken its toll. Any more talk would have to wait. It was time for both of them to get some sleep.

He brushed his lips against hers and said good-night, convinced the fiery redhead would haunt his dreams.

Chapter Eleven

Alerted to the herd's arrival, tourists lined the fences along the final drive into Kissimmee on Monday morning. Riders who had slouched their way through ten days and one hundred and twenty miles sat tall in their saddles. They whistled and wore wide smiles. Long, braided leather whips snapped sharply, their signature crack echoing for miles and earning the wielders the right to be called Florida Crackers. Dust stirred by hundreds of hooves clouded the air. Horses whinnied. Their eyes wide, brown-sided cattle streamed through the gate and into the pens outside the Kissimmee Sports Arena. In another two months, the area would all but burst at the seams with livestock used in the Silver Spurs Rodeo. But on a warm day in January, Ty's crew practically had the place to themselves.

"Fifty head of prime beef cattle." The rail-thin manager of the cow pens marked his tally on a clipboard as the gate swung shut behind the last of the herd. "You say they're shipping out tomorrow? Where they headed? Stockyards?"

If Sarah didn't know Ty so well, she might have missed the slight tightening of the skin along his jawline.

"Nah," he said. "These are feeder cows, intended

to build a herd in North Florida. The buyer's trucks'll be here in the morning. Till then, I expect you to take good care of them."

"You have my word." The manager stuck out his free hand, and Ty shook it. If he cared that the cows born and raised on his ranch would live out their lives so far from home, it didn't show in the relaxed set of Ty's shoulders.

Ignoring the pockets of his quilted jacket, the older man stuck one hand in his jeans pocket, the clipboard tucked under his arm. He aimed his chin toward Lacy. The cow stood, tail swishing, tied to the back of the chuck wagon. "I take it the Brahman's not part of the shipment? You want me to take her off your hands?"

When Ty appeared to give this offer some thought, Sarah shot him a questioning look. She let her gaze drop pointedly to the little boy at her side, the one who would be crushed if Ty sold the cow.

The rancher pulled the brim of his hat down low. One corner of his mouth twitched. Behind his sunglasses, he winked at her.

"We'll take her back to the Circle P with us," he said at last. "That calf she's carrying belongs to Tompkins if it turns out to be a Brahman. But I'd be much obliged if you'd let her stay in one of the pens while we have lunch and trailer the horses." Even as he spoke, Seth and the crew were loading their gear into trucks for the long drive back to the ranch.

"You sure?" The cattleman thrust an accusatory thumb toward the cow. "She's gonna cost ya more than she's worth in vet bills and feed. That calf turns out to be a mixed-breed, you know you'll only wind up takin' it to Hayes."

Familiar with the family-owned butcher shop, Sarah

sucked in a breath. She cast a worried glance at Jimmy. If he ever thought Lacy or her calf might wind up on someone's dinner plate…well, the idea was enough to make a vegetarian out of a little boy who refused to eat anything green. Fortunately, the cattle that now milled about in the pens had Jimmy's rapt attention. Sarah breathed a sigh of relief.

"Sorry," Ty said with a bit more firmness. "The tyke's taken a shine to her." He placed a hand on the boy's shoulder. "If it turns out the calf's not full Brahman, I thought it might be a good idea for him to raise it. He'll be in 4-H soon enough and might as well get some experience."

While the men finalized their arrangements, tears stung at the corners of Sarah's eyes. She swiped at them, hoping no one would notice. Every time she thought she had Ty figured out, he did something that proved her wrong. She loved Ty in a way she'd never loved anyone before. And he was so sexy, so handsome, that she could hardly wait until they returned to the ranch and spent their first night together. As for the future, she'd meant it when she said they'd take it one step at a time, but she had no doubt they'd be taking those steps side by side for the rest of their lives. The man of her dreams wanted to build a future with her. He'd offered to let her open a plant nursery on the Circle P.

And now, for her sake, Ty had shouldered responsibility for Jimmy. Wasn't convincing him to raise the child the reason she'd come to the Circle P in the first place? From what he'd just said, Ty had every intention of doing that. His change of heart should have made her the happiest person on the face of the earth.

What, then, was the fly in the ointment of her happiness?

Her gaze fell from the chiseled features that made her pulse race to the child who looked just like him. Despite Ty's willingness to raise the boy, unease whispered in her ear. Jimmy deserved to be cherished and loved in his own right, not raised as "Sarah's kid." An afterthought. An appendage.

If only the man she loved had claimed the boy as his own….

But she had to face facts. It wasn't going to happen. Ty had wedged himself in too deep to change his mind without proof. She'd just have to trust that once the lab results came in, he'd finally acknowledge the boy as his own flesh and blood.

A buzz vibrated from the cell phone that had hung uselessly from her waist for the past week. For a second, Sarah hesitated, unwilling to let the everyday world, with all its demands and problems, intrude on the idyllic time she'd spent on the cattle drive. Insistent, her phone buzzed again and, with a sigh, she flipped it open. Beneath the broad banner of an incoming call, text messages and emails scrolled across the screen. She barely glanced at them before lifting the phone to her ear. "This is Sarah."

"Why haven't you been answering my calls? I must have left a dozen messages."

At Connie's frantic chatter, Sarah's shoulders automatically stiffened. She made a conscious effort to relax them. Signaling Ty to watch Jimmy, she strode a few yards down the dusty trail she'd so recently traveled.

"I told you I'd be out of reach until the cattle drive arrived in Kissimmee," she said when she'd put enough distance between her and Ty to ensure privacy.

"This place has turned into an absolute zoo without you. No one knows where anything is. The transition to the new computer system has been a disaster. We need you in the office, pronto. How soon are you coming back?"

At the unfamiliar panic in Connie's voice, Sarah suppressed a bitter smile. For years, she'd worked days, nights and weekends to earn the promotion she'd been promised. Now that her supervisor had finally realized how indispensible she'd become, Sarah no longer wanted the job. But telling her boss that she planned to extend her leave indefinitely…that wasn't a conversation she wanted to have over the phone.

"I still have a few vacation days on the books," she hedged. "I'll see you next week."

"Well." With one word, Connie conveyed both dissatisfaction and resignation. "In the meantime, we can't find the file on the Baxter boy."

Sarah pictured the young man who'd spent most of his life bouncing from one home to another. In celebration of Tony Baxter's eighteenth birthday and the end of his stipend from the state, his latest set of foster parents had notified the DCF that he could no longer live with them. Her last official act before leaving the office had been to arrange transitional housing for the boy.

"I've reserved his place at Genesis House." The group home was in the same district as Tony's school, making it possible for the high school senior to graduate with his friends. "All the paperwork is in his file. Look in the top drawer of my file cabinet."

"These kids have been aging out of the system at eighteen for as long as I've been with the DCF. He could have managed on his own."

Sarah bristled at Connie's brusque tone, but she didn't say a word. She didn't have to. She and Connie had clashed more than once about the state's policy of putting teenagers on the street with little more than the clothes on their backs and best wishes for a happy life. Few made the transition successfully, and no wonder. Even kids from homes where there were two loving parents had problems staying in school and out of trouble. How was anyone supposed to do it on their own?

At last, Connie sighed into the silence. "I guess we'll go ahead with your plans."

Sarah barely had time to be grateful before her boss switched subjects. "And how are things going with the Parker boy and his father?"

"Better than I expected, actually." Sarah cast a glance over her shoulder. Ty and Jimmy stood with their backs to her, the little boy's hand firmly in the tall rancher's grip.

"Good. Then you'll be leaving the child with him when you return?"

Yes, she agreed before ending the call. She'd leave Jimmy with Ty. But only for a short while. Just long enough to check on her plants and fill a suitcase with something other than jeans and T-shirts for her stay at the ranch.

Sarah had nearly put the phone away when a cheery ping alerted her to an incoming email. She thumbed the screen and hit the delete key. Another spam message landed in her trash folder.

There were other, more important messages to deal with, though, and she quickly scrolled through them. Her finger paused over an official-looking notification from the DCF lab where Jimmy and Ty had had their blood drawn. A pleasant thrill raced through Sarah's midsection. Eager to put any lingering doubts about

Jimmy's parentage to rest before she and Ty started their new life together, she stabbed at the email.

At the words "Tyrone Parker is excluded," black spots danced before her eyes. She blinked them away and stared in disbelief at the message. Ty was not Jimmy's father. Her vision swam. She couldn't catch her breath. Struggling for tiny sips of air, she cupped a hand over the moan that threatened to escape her lips.

Unable to resist, she stole another glimpse of Ty and Jimmy. Sure, the boy didn't have Ty's broad shoulders, but in every other aspect he was a miniature version of the rancher, right down to the color of his hair. How was it possible the two weren't father and son?

And how would Ty react when he learned the truth?

There was only one way to find out and, straightening her shoulders, Sarah headed toward the fence rail where the two people she loved most watched the milling cattle.

"Ty?" The word barely whispered through her suddenly parched lips. She licked them and tried again. "Ty, I need to tell you some—"

But it was Jimmy who first swung to face her. "Miss Sarah! Did you know we're going to Mr. Ty's ranch? And we're bringing Lacy? She's going to be my very own cow. I get to feed her and brush her. All by myself."

Ty settled his long fingers across the youngster's shoulders. "Not till you're a bit bigger, pardner. You need to eat lots of Ms. Doris's cooking and grow another couple of inches. Meantime, we'll do things together. Want to go for another ride on Ranger tonight?"

"Yes, please, Mr. Ty!" Pure, unadulterated hero worship glistened in Jimmy's gaze.

"Blood will tell. Blood always tells," Ty had said on more than one occasion.

Sarah bit down hard on her bottom lip, her thoughts racing. For her sake, Ty had resigned himself to the fact that she and the boy were a package deal, but no one could expect the rancher to raise his wife's love child. Even if he was the bravest, most compassionate man Sarah had ever known.

Her plan to share the results of the DNA test stuttered and she gulped. How could she ruin this moment for the little boy who had wormed his way into her heart? Or rob him of his only chance to visit the Circle P? She couldn't. Not now.

No, she wouldn't lie to Ty, wouldn't withhold the truth from him. At least, not for long. But her news could wait for a day or two. Until she had a chance to put another plan into motion. One that didn't include a future on the Circle P. Or tall, handsome ranchers.

Stunned, Sarah stood for a moment. She scanned the cows in their pens, the ranch hands loading equipment into trucks, the people she'd spent time with, the man she'd fallen in love with despite their short time together. In a world that no longer made sense, there was only one choice open to her. As much as it killed her to do it, she tugged her hat down low and pushed her sunglasses firmly into place.

"Change of plans," she announced loud enough to muffle her breaking heart. "Something's come up. Would you mind taking Jimmy back to the Circle P alone?"

Behind her dark glasses, Sarah swallowed tears at the disappointment that flitted across Ty's face. Her resolve wavered. One look at the excited little boy at his side, though, and she forced herself to stay strong.

She built a dam around the tears that sprang from her breaking heart while she explained that an emergency required her immediate return to Fort Pierce.

"Everything okay?" Concern puckered Ty's brow.

"Yes. No. A work thing." Her fingers crossed, she waved her phone. "I'll be gone a day, two at the most."

Though she nearly faltered beneath Ty's questioning gaze, she stuck to her story and made sure he knew how to reach her if need be. As the social worker assigned to Jimmy's case, she couldn't adopt the boy. Her involvement was too much a conflict of interest. But there was nothing on the books to prevent a *former* DCF worker from fostering a child. She'd turn in her resignation and apply for guardianship in one fell swoop. It wouldn't take long, just a couple of days. Two days would give her enough time to work out the details of her new life before she returned to the Circle P to claim the boy and tell Ty the truth.

At last the rancher nodded, and she turned her back. Her eyes blurred with tears that were far different from the ones she'd cried earlier. She swept them away and checked her watch. If she caught the first ride back to the Circle P, she could pick up her car and make the two-hour drive to Fort Pierce before dark. Once she put her plan to adopt Jimmy in motion and checked on her plants which, Matt and Elliott's advice to the contrary, would be her only source of income for the foreseeable future, she'd return to tell Ty he was off the hook. She took a steadying breath and turned to look one last time at the life she was leaving behind.

As though they'd rehearsed the move, Ty and Jimmy swung to face her. They doffed their hats. At Ty's beckoning wave, Sarah squared her shoulders and straightened her spine. Ten minutes later, she slid onto the seat beside Doris while she pondered the things she hadn't told the man she loved.

He'd been right about that blood thing all along. Blood told. And this time, it spelled the end of their future together. Turning to stare out the window, Sarah made no effort to staunch the silent tears that slid down her cheeks.

THE WESTERN SKY GLOWED pink and gold by the time Sarah pulled onto the driveway beside a modest cement-block home in an older Fort Pierce neighborhood. She squinted at her lawn. An unnatural pall colored the blades of grass. Her throat tightened. If the hardy St. Augustine had died, temperatures must have plunged lower than she'd anticipated. Her heart in her throat, she focused on the front porch where the orchid she'd babied for ten years hung, browned and ugly, from the planter near the door.

"No. Oh, no," she whispered. She wrenched open the car door and stumbled up the walk. A darkened leaf crumbled at her touch. Flakes drifted down. They landed atop a soggy pile of ruined blossoms.

Feeling sick to her stomach, Sarah fumbled in her purse. Her fingers shook so badly, it took three tries before she rammed the key home. The door sprang open.

Along the windowsill, stalks of the plumeria she'd been rooting in glass jars slumped like wilted celery. She rushed onto the back porch. Stacks of blankets and towels proved the sitter had at least tried to save her plants. But everywhere Sarah looked, absolute devastation stared back at her.

The vibrant greens of once-healthy plants had given way to browned and blackened leaves. Colorless blossoms littered the floor beneath hanging plants that were now nothing more than bare, lifeless twigs. Not a single orchid had survived the cold. Sarah closed her eyes. She swung toward the beds that had been filled with gorgeous yellow, red and pink blossoms less than two weeks earlier. When she squinted a look, a single green twig stood among the blackened branches, the only survivor from her prize-winning flowers. She leaned down and pressed it gently only to feel the husk collapse at her touch.

The discovery robbed her of breath and coherent thought. Sarah sank to the floor. She sifted black dirt through her fingers and sighed.

She should have listened to Matt and Elliott. They'd tried to warn her that supporting herself with a plant nursery was ludicrous. Only Ty had believed in the concept—and in her—enough to help make her plans a reality.

Not that it mattered.

Her plants were as dead as any hope of a future with Ty. He'd made how he felt about raising another man's son perfectly clear. And the proof that Millie had been unfaithful would develop into hurt and frustration. Sarah knew that Ty wouldn't have to lift a finger or say one unkind word to make the boy feel unwanted, unloved. She'd seen it happen too many times. She wouldn't, she couldn't let Jimmy grow up in an environment where his very existence was resented.

Sarah took a steadying breath. Okay, so she'd suffered a blow. Two of them, actually. She still had work to do, still had Jimmy's future to secure. Tomorrow, she'd resign her position with the DCF and start the ball rolling to adopt the boy. It wasn't as if she didn't have resources. She had savings. It might not be much, but it'd see them through until she found a new job.

Now, if only she could envision a future without a certain broad-shouldered rancher, Sarah knew she'd be okay. Trouble was, she couldn't.

TY RAN A HAND OVER HIS FACE. Acid burned in the pit of his stomach as he leaned on the top rail of Lacy's stall and stared down at the cow's prone form. The wide gray sides had stopped heaving an hour earlier, minutes after she'd given birth to a tawny Brahma/Andalusia mix.

Kneeling on a fresh bed of straw, Seth finished giving the tiny calf a vigorous rubdown and patted it gently on its rump. "If you're gonna keep her, we need to get a couple 'a bottles of colostrum into this little gal soon's we can." Ordinarily, the newborn would get much-needed nutrients and antibodies from its mother. Not an option for this orphan.

Ty saw the questions in Seth's tired eyes, met them and nodded. Lacy's death would hit Jimmy hard enough. To lose the calf, too… Well, he couldn't do that to the boy.

"We'll keep her. I'll call the vet first thing in the morning. Meantime, are the boys on the lookout for a surrogate? I'd hate to have to bottle-raise her." Bottle feeding was a labor-intensive proposition, one reserved only for calves that were worth the effort.

"Already taken care of." Seth wiped his hands on the towel and stood. "Josh found a heifer moonin' over her dead calf in the back pasture. He's bringing her in now. We'll see if we can't trick her into believing this young'un's hers."

"You gonna try the talc?" Cows identified their calves by smell. A liberal dusting of talcum powder often disguised the orphan's odor long enough to fool the surrogate into nursing it. Once the mother bonded with its new baby, the talc went back on the shelf, ready for the next time.

"Yep." Seth slugged coffee from the cup Ty had brought him. "It'll be light soon. That boy'll be up. What you gonna tell him?"

Ty hitched his mouth to one side and forced air through his nose. For the umpteenth time in twenty-four hours, he wished Sarah hadn't been called back to Fort Pierce. If anyone would know how to handle the situation, she would. He sure didn't. The best he could do was hope that Sarah returned before he had to have a heart-to-heart chat with the boy.

"I'll keep him busy this morning while you and the boys clean up this mess." A sigh escaped his lips while he gestured to the stall with one hand. "No need to let him see the—" thinking of Jimmy's forlorn little face, *carcass* seemed too harsh "—body. Later I'll introduce him to the calf and hope he doesn't think to ask about..." He paused. There were good reasons they didn't name the cows on the ranch. This was one of them. "About Lacy," he finished.

It took a bit of the old soft shoe, but over breakfast, Ty danced around Jimmy's questions about the pregnant cow. "We'll go out to the barn later," he said as they took their places at the kitchen table. "For now, I thought we could start cleaning out the old greenhouse so Ms. Sarah can use it for her flowers. I want to surprise her by having it all done when she gets back. What do you think?"

"She likes flowers. She has lots of pretty ones at her house." Jimmy chewed thoughtfully on the biscuit he'd all but crammed in his mouth. "I think she'd like that." He pushed away from the table. "I'll get my boots."

"Whoa, pardner," Ty cautioned. "Let's slow down and finish our breakfast. We'll let our food settle a bit before we go rushing out the door." While they ate, several of the ranch hands were rolling new, heavy-duty plastic over the frame of the greenhouse. Ty wanted every hammer and nail safely secured before Jimmy took one step into the place.

The little boy shrugged and slid his feet back under the table. "Sure, Mr. Ty." He reached for a second biscuit. "Could I have the jelly, please?"

An hour later, Jimmy and Doris made short work of pulling dried vines from the trellises and yanking the brown skeletons of long-dead plants from the potting trays in a greenhouse that smelled like fresh plastic. While Ty checked out the plumbing and sprinkler systems, his helpers scooped dirt from flower beds and swept the floor clean. By late morning, the greenhouse had started to take shape.

Ty whistled as he installed the latches on a new door. He'd oiled the hinges and replaced the lock when footsteps sounded on the bare concrete behind him. "Hey, there. Where you going with all those?" he asked, holding the door wide to let Jimmy pass.

The boy tottered out of the greenhouse carrying a stack of clay pots nearly as high as he was tall. "They was all on the table. You said we had to take everything outside. I'm helpin'."

The stack of pots tilted precariously. One fell from the top, hit the dirt and rolled out of sight.

"Oops!"

"I see that you're helpin', pardner." Knowing he sported a goofy grin, Ty hurried to the boy's aid. "Best let me help, too, or every one of those pots will get smashed to smithereens."

Jimmy peered up at him while Ty took the stack from his hands. "Smithereens," he said rolling the sounds around in his mouth. "I like that word. Tonight, I'm gonna mash my vegetables to smithereens."

Ty's grin deepened. He still couldn't believe he'd been lucky enough to find the love of his life and a son in a matter of weeks. No, the child wasn't his blood, but every boy needed a father figure. He wanted to be that man for Jimmy. After gently placing the pots on the ground, he ran a hand through the kid's hair. "Good job," he said.

Turning, he studied all they'd accomplished in the short while since breakfast. Beside him, Jimmy turned, too, and folded his arms across his chest the same way Ty had.

"Ms. Sarah will like this," the boy announced.

"I think so," Ty agreed. But now that they'd removed all the dirt and trash, the plant trays looked a little bare. He dusted his hands on his jeans. There was plenty of time to visit the nursery down the road where he could buy potting soil and such. He was reaching for the keys to the truck when he spotted Seth across the yard. The manager waved an all-clear signal, letting him know everything in the barn had been squared away.

Ty turned toward Jimmy. "You want to see Lacy's new calf?"

Jimmy's eyes widened. Wonder filled his little boy voice. "She had a baby?"

"Sure did. A little heifer. She's in the barn."

Before Ty had a chance to say another word, Jimmy took off. He ran straight as an arrow, his boots pounding the hard-packed dirt of the yard between the main house and the stables. Ty caught up with him at the doorway, which was easily wide enough to accommodate a tractor.

"Hey, now," he said. "Let's be quiet inside." He was probably taking the coward's way out, but he couldn't bring himself to tell the boy the whole story. He placed a hand on the child's shoulder and guided him to the stall.

Jimmy looped his fingers over a board. His mouth gaped open as he stared through the opening between the slats. Ty braced for questions. When they didn't come, he shrugged and joined the boy at the rail.

Against one wall, the tiny calf nuzzled its adoptive mom. At first, all Ty saw were the differences between the tawny youngster and the dark brown Andalusian with its flat chest and stubby horns. Loose folds of skin hung from the little one's neck. They would eventually develop into a heavy Brahman dewlap. But instead of flopping down like those of Jar Jar Binks in *Star Wars,* the calf's ears perked up like those of every other cow on the Circle P.

Ty swallowed a curse. The calf's parentage couldn't be more obvious.

"She's real pretty," Jimmy whispered.

Pretty was not the word Ty would have chosen, but he figured in this case the old adage about beauty being in the eye of the beholder held true.

"Why is she in with that other mama cow?" Jimmy stared up at him, wonder at the newborn still etched on his face. "Where's Lacy?"

Ty took a deep breath. Much as he hated to be the bearer of bad news, sometimes being a parent meant exactly that. Squatting in front of the boy, he gazed into Jimmy's trusting brown eyes. "I'm afraid Lacy got very sick after the calf was born. She was an old cow. Too old to have a baby. And she died."

"She's not here?" Jimmy's searching gaze took in the entire barn. At last, his eyes met Ty's again. "Is she in heaven with my mom?"

Ty swallowed. He was a cattleman, not a philosopher. He gave the boy the best answer he could find. "Yeah, pardner, I guess she is."

Jimmy shrugged his thin shoulders in a gesture far too adult for a five-year-old. "My mom will look out for Lacy. She needs a friend while she's up there and I'm here."

Ty's throat tightened and he bobbed his head, unable to find even the simplest of words. For a while, they watched the calf and her adoptive mom in silence. Jimmy poked a couple of pieces of hay into the stall, trying to tempt the baby closer without any luck. According to Seth, the Andalusian had taken to the newborn right away. Blood might be everything to some, but it obviously didn't affect this pair, and Ty was struck at how easily the two had bonded.

He forced his gaze from the nursing calf to Jimmy and back again, then rubbed his eyes as the last niggling doubts about the boy faded into nothingness. Though Sarah was certain he was Jimmy's father, Ty was just as certain he wasn't. But in the grand scheme of things, what did it matter? Whether he had created the child or not, he'd be a real dad to the boy. He cleared his throat.

"Time for lunch?" he asked. "I could get into a couple of peanut butter and jelly sandwiches."

Jimmy rubbed his stomach. "Me, too." On their way out of the barn, the little boy tipped his head. "Mr. Ty?"

"Yeah, pardner?"

"I'm glad the calf found a new mom."

Ty blinked at a sudden dampness at the corners of his eyes. "Me, too, little man," he whispered. "Me, too."

He scanned the road that would bring Sarah back to the Circle P, back to his arms, back to the little boy who needed a mom as well as a dad. No matter how hard he stared, not so much as a smudge marred the horizon above an endless stretch of flat land. Convinced Sarah wasn't going to arrive at the ranch anytime soon, he crossed his fingers, hoping things had gone well for her in Fort Pierce. What she was doing there, he wasn't quite sure. Her abrupt departure in the middle of the herd's arrival in Kissimmee had left too little time for questions. He supposed whatever had come up at the DCF office was keeping her busy. Too busy to return the messages he'd left on her cell phone.

He shrugged aside a nagging uncertainty. Had she realized that a future with him wasn't what she wanted after all? Had she decided, like Millie, that life on the ranch would be too boring, too isolated? He shook his head. Sarah wasn't Millie. She'd promised to return to the Circle P by nightfall. And before her arrival there were things to do, a little boy to feed and potting soil to buy for the greenhouse he intended as her welcome home present.

Chapter Twelve

While Jimmy lingered over lunch to tell Doris all about the new calf, Ty excused himself. A small mountain of mail had piled up while he was busy with the cattle drive. It demanded his attention. In the den, he sorted the advertisements and fliers from the bills. Those he dealt into separate stacks. One for feed and the vet's services. Household expenses into another. Halfway through, his eyes narrowed at an envelope from an unfamiliar lab. It took a second for understanding to register.

The paternity test results. Had to be.

Reaching for the letter opener, he sank slowly into his chair. A single sheet of paper slid out of the envelope. He fanned it open on the desk. And stared.

He'd seen enough DNA tests on horses and cows to know immediately that something was off. Sure enough, the results stared up at him from the bottom of the page.

"Tyrone Parker is excluded as the biological father of James Tyrone Parker."

The peanut butter and jelly sandwich he'd wolfed down with Jimmy threatened to make a return appearance.

Ty drew in a thready breath. And then another. This wasn't unexpected, he told himself. He'd known all along the child wasn't his. He took a minute to absorb the news before deciding it didn't matter what the report said. Legally, Jimmy was still his son. Unless some unknown person stepped forward…

Ty stopped. He scanned the info at the top of the page, his stomach tightening at the bold *X* beside Sarah's name and email address. He rubbed a spot that had begun hurting below his rib cage. Was that why she'd left for Fort Pierce with barely a word? Was she, even now, starting an investigation to find Jimmy's biological father?

If so, he had no one to blame but himself. The end of the cattle drive was always a pleasantly hectic time. He'd talked to each of his guests, invited them back for another visit, seen them off to the airport. Horses and gear were loaded onto trailers for the long drive back to the Circle P. A million other details required attention, including the special handling of a very pregnant cow. With all that going on, he hadn't found the time to discuss his decision about the boy with Sarah. He'd planned to do that tonight. Now, he wondered if he was too late.

He reached for the phone and dialed her number. When there was no answer on Sarah's cell, he left a message. And one at her house. And another one on her office phone.

Flipping his cell phone end over end, he pondered what to do next. It didn't take long to decide he needed to do something to show his change of heart.

"Jimmy," he called. "C'mon in here."

The sound of little boots clomping down the hallway brought a smile to Ty's face.

"Yes, Mr. Ty?" the child said from the doorway.

"Remember when you caught your first fish?" At the boy's nod, he continued, "Come help me print out the picture. We'll hang it on the wall." Ty paused. Was he really going to do this? He took a breath and finished what he'd started. "With all the other family photographs."

With Jimmy pushing the buttons on his computer, it look a little longer than usual to transfer the best of several shots from his phone to the hard drive and print copies. While the ink set, he scrounged around in the office until he found an empty frame. Slipping Jimmy's picture inside, he held the boy's hand and guided him to the gallery of photos that recorded the history of the Circle P.

Ty pointed to a faded black-and-white print of the bearded patriarch.

"That's my great-grandfather, Tyrone Parker the first. He bought this land a long time ago. Four generations of Parkers have lived in this house and raised cattle on this ranch."

Jimmy tilted his head back. He squinted at the picture. "Hey," he said. "We have the same last name. I'm James Tyrone Parker."

"I know that, pardner." Ty gave the little boy's hand a squeeze. "My name's Tyrone Parker, too. Most people call me Ty, just like most people call you Jimmy."

Step by step, they moved toward the end of the hall with Ty stopping to identify the figures in each picture. He didn't come right out and connect the dots for the boy. There'd be time enough for that once he tied all the legal details into a neat bow.

"Who are those boys?" Jimmy asked when they

reached the most recent photos. "Do they live here? Can I play with them?"

"That's me when I was a little older than you are now." Ty tapped a picture of himself standing in the kitchen of the Circle P, his head freshly shaved. He pointed to a nearly identical figure seated on a stool. Hair, some dark and some light, littered the floor. "That's my best friend, J.D."

"Why'd you cut off all your hair?"

"We'd just gotten our buzz cuts for the summer. It's cooler that way. Summers are hot."

Ty laughed out loud when Jimmy raised his hands protectively over his own blond head. His chuckles tapered off as memories of his childhood friend flooded back. Two peas in a pod, Doris had called them, but they hadn't really been because J.D.'s hair had always been the color of corn silk while his own hadn't lightened until the sun bleached it. His gaze dropped to the little boy in the hallway. The one who looked so much like him. The one whose blond hair was not sun bleached.

Millie and J.D.?

With an *oof* Ty stumbled back a step.

He shook his head, unable to accept in his heart the truth his mind had known all along. All the questions he'd had since the day Sarah had called him into her office, all the answers he'd been seeking fell into place. J.D.'s insistence that Millie was wrong for him finally made sense...if his best friend had wanted her for himself. The odd tension that had filled the house the summer before J.D. shipped out. Ty had attributed it to being on edge over his friend's orders to Afghanistan. He rubbed his temples where a headache threatened. No wonder Millie hadn't told him about the baby.

How do you explain that you've had an affair with your husband's best friend? It's easier to run away, especially when…

Ty waved a hand, trying to ward off the image of solemn, uniformed men stepping from a black car in front of the Circle P.

He needed air, and with Jimmy excitedly pointing to the spot he wanted for his picture, Ty knew he couldn't take much more.

"Stay here," he growled. Leaving the boy, he walked to the end of the hall where he drew in several deep breaths.

When he could finally breathe again and the walls no longer seemed like they were closing in on him, Ty checked his gut. He expected to feel a sense of betrayal. Instead, regret floated at the top of his swirling emotions. Regret that his best friend had died, never knowing he had a son. Sorrow that he and Millie hadn't been able to mourn J.D.'s passing together. He wished she'd confided in him. Sure, he would have been upset. He might have even railed for a while. But they'd have worked it out. For J.D.'s sake, if for no other.

Tears burned the back of Ty's throat. He brushed a hand over his eyes. There was no changing what had happened six years ago. The question was, how did he move forward?

"Mr. Ty?" Jimmy's hand tugged on his shirtsleeve. "Mr. Ty, are you okay?"

Looking down, Ty realized the boy was due for a trim. He squatted down until he was face-to-face with the child whose name should have been his first clue. James Tyrone Parker. Son of James Dalton, known to all who loved him as J.D. He stared into the boy's troubled dark brown eyes and saw his best friend staring back at him.

"Yeah, kiddo," he said, brushing the kid's hair off his forehead. "I'm okay. How 'bout we hang that picture and then we'll ask Ms. Doris to rustle us up some ice cream."

A toothy grin spread across Jimmy's face, and in an instant, J.D. was gone.

Ty nodded. There'd come a time when the kid was old enough to start asking questions. When he did, Ty vowed to tell him the truth. But for now, the little boy deserved to have pictures of his mom hanging in the hallway. Ty took a breath, knowing he'd have to dig one or two out of the box in the back of his closet.

But that, too, could wait.

For now, he had to drive to Fort Pierce and set things right with Sarah. Had she seen the DNA test and bolted? Did she plan to throw the boy into the system? Dread filled his chest with the idea that she might.

He had to get to her, to make sure she hadn't done the thing he feared. Especially now that she was apparently refusing to return his phone calls. After making hasty arrangements with Seth and Doris to watch Jimmy, Ty aimed his pickup truck toward Fort Pierce and hit the gas, hoping he wasn't too late.

AFTER SPENDING every day in fresh air and sunshine on Ty's ranch, slipping into a suit felt like getting fitted for a straitjacket. But showing up at the DCF office in a T-shirt and jeans wouldn't win Sarah any points with her boss. And she needed Connie on her side. So, much as she preferred her broken-in cowboy boots, Sarah put on a sturdy pair of sling-backs. Then she tamed her curls, pinning and spraying every strand into a tight bun. Convinced she'd done all she could to make a good impression, she checked her reflection in the mirror.

Red-rimmed eyes and a deathly pale complexion really weren't her best look. She was stuck with them, though. At least until a certain rancher faded from her thoughts.

Sarah shook her head. Who was she kidding? She'd never forget Ty. She couldn't go a single minute without longing to feel his strong arms about her, without wishing she could press her head against his chest, listen to his steady heartbeat. He'd kept her warm, made her laugh, risked his life for hers. Envisioning a future without him was harder than she'd ever imagined it would be and, not for the first time, she questioned whether she'd made the right decision by leaving.

The answer, as always, came back to Jimmy. Much as she loved Ty, she'd vowed to protect the child. If that meant raising him as a single parent rather than exposing him to a lifetime of resentment, she had to do it. No matter how much it broke her heart.

But what if…

She'd misjudged Ty?

He'd changed?

Sarah closed her eyes, shutting off an avenue of thought that would only delay her heartbreak, not heal it. She'd made a decision. For the sake of the child, she'd live by it.

Standing, she gathered her carefully crafted resignation and the adoption application in hands that barely trembled and headed for her car. She pulled into a crowded parking lot minutes later. Inside the DCF office, clients occupied every available chair while children ran riot through the play area. Sarah walked past cubicles where grumbling coworkers hunched over their keyboards. She steeled herself against the urge to pitch in and help out by reminding herself she'd come here for a purpose. Until she'd accomplished it, she couldn't think about anything else.

She nearly made it to Connie's office before her nerve faltered. Quickly she reiterated all the reasons why quitting her job, adopting a son and walking away from the love of her life made sense. Though her heart wasn't nearly as sure as her head, Sarah kept her feet in motion. She rapped on Connie's door.

"Welcome back," her boss said with a frown.

When Connie looked up from her monitor, Sarah noted the dark circles under her eyes and gave her the benefit of the doubt. The woman played hunt-and-peck with the keyboard, the look of consternation on her face deepening until Sarah offered a tentative "Need some help?"

"How are your computer skills?" Connie pushed away from her desk. "I spent most of last night trying to compile a list of foster kids in our care. No luck."

Glad for the opportunity to make one last contribution to the DCF, Sarah reached over and, with a few keystrokes, produced the desired information. One more jab of the mouse, and the printer in the corner of the room began to chatter.

"It's about time." Connie sighed. "Just between you and me, this new system hasn't lived up to my expectations."

Sarah understood her boss well enough to know the remark was the closest she'd ever come to hearing a thank-you.

"Let me guess. Everyone's spending too much time entering data for reports that aren't easy to run?" Sarah had tried to point out the flaws while they were in the design phase. She nodded to the computer. "Is that why the parking lot is full and the waiting room is bursting at the seams?"

Connie hiked one eyebrow. Apparently remembering the new system was her baby, one she and Sarah had argued about on more than one occasion, she folded her arms across her chest. "I'm sure once everyone reads the manual, things will smooth out."

Sarah eyed the thick instruction book. "I've said all along, we need more staff. Not expensive software. Still, I hope you're right." She managed a sympathetic smile. What she had to say wasn't going to make Connie's life easier. "Actually, I'm here because of the Parker boy," she began.

"Oh?" Another raised eyebrow. "I thought that was all settled."

"I thought so, too, but..." Sarah took a deep breath. "Mr. Parker never accepted Jimmy as his son. Not from the very beginning. He..." Miserable, she studied her feet. She'd been so sure Ty was the boy's father, she'd never mentioned the paternity test to Connie. She should have. Now she had no choice.

"He had their DNA tested. The results came in. He's been right all along."

"And this is the first I'm hearing of it?" Anger flashed in Connie's eyes. "Wait. We'll get to that in a minute." She removed her glasses and set them aside. "You couldn't convince him to raise the boy. He's giving up his rights to the child?"

Ty had made his stance abundantly clear. "He will. But I have a solution. I want to adopt Jimmy."

Disbelief filled Connie's expression. "You've got to be kidding."

Sarah straightened her shoulders. "After the rough

start he's had, the boy deserves someone who'll always be there for him. I can be that person."

Connie waved this last part aside as if it were of no consequence. "It would smack of impropriety, of special treatment, if a parent gave up their rights to a child and then his caseworker adopted him. We have strict guidelines against such things."

"They don't prevent a *former* DCF worker from adopting a child." Sarah slid the papers she'd prepared across the desk.

Connie eyed the sheets the way someone might look at a germ-laden tissue. Gingerly, she picked the first one up by its corner. She stared down at Sarah's resignation. When she looked up again, disappointment deepened the wrinkles in her lined face.

"I've known for some time you weren't the right person to take my place when I retire." She sighed. "Regretfully, I accept your resignation."

Hearing the relief in her boss's voice, Sarah exhaled slowly. For more than a year she'd suspected empty promises had lured her to Fort Pierce. Though it stung to know she'd invested so much of herself in a job that had never been within her reach, having Jimmy in her life made the sacrifice worth the effort. She leaned forward, tapped the second piece of paper. "Now that I'm no longer employed by DCF, there's no impediment to my application for temporary custody of James Parker."

Connie pursed her lips as though she'd been sucking on a sour lemon. She turned the sheet, facedown, on the desk. "I can't approve it."

Sarah fought to remain calm. Was this some kind of test? If so, she was determined to pass it. "You can't possibly doubt that I'd make a good home for the child."

She was, after all, a social worker entrusted with responsibility for hundreds of foster kids.

Or at least, she had been until two minutes ago.

Yellow tabs fluttered along the edges when Connie thumbed a worn copy of the DCF rule book. "We are in a unique position with regard to the children under our care," she said as if quoting from the text. "Adoption by a former caseworker might not be prohibited, but the higher-ups will never allow it. If I approved your application, it would only get your hopes up. There's no sense in that."

Sarah's gaze shifted from a manual filled with arcane policies that, in her opinion, focused too much on paperwork and not nearly enough on children, to the woman whose approval she needed. "But what about Jimmy?" she asked, her voice wavering.

"I imagine he'll have a rough time at first—they all do—but a few weeks in The Glades will toughen him up. We'll move him to a foster home as soon as we can."

Sarah's head swam. "You'd rather put a five-year-old in a group home or foster care, than let him live with me? Someone who loves him?"

"I'm sorry," Connie said. "But rules are rules. I can't make an exception because you've gotten close to this child."

Disbelief rose in Sarah's throat. She swallowed. Her stomach clenched at the thought of never seeing the little boy again.

"I have always had the best interest of the child at heart," she insisted.

"True, but you've gotten too involved." Connie shook her head. "That's always been your downfall—getting too involved."

"That's where we differ." Sarah squared her shoulders. "I consider it one of my strengths. This isn't over. I'll appeal your decision. Fight you in court." It might take longer than she'd planned, but she would win. For Jimmy's sake, she had to win.

"You'd best forget all about James Parker. Believe me, one day you'll thank me for denying your application."

Sarah thought her ex-boss looked far too confident for someone who, five minutes earlier, hadn't been able to wrestle so much as a simple report from the new computer system. The system Connie had insisted would solve all of the DCF's problems. But arguing with the woman was pointless. Pulling the unraveled edges of her composure together, she managed a calm "I'll clean out my office right away" and left without another word.

In her office, she filled a cardboard box with the few personal items that had brightened the otherwise claustrophobic space. Tears stung at her eyes as she pulled open her desk drawer. Staring down at the yellow legal pad where she'd scribbled her few notes about Jimmy, she blinked. Even as her heart stuttered, her vision cleared. Her fingers trembling, Sarah slid the notepad into the box.

Judging by the overflowing parking lot, the crowded waiting room, the complaints of her former coworkers, Connie would have her hands full for the next few days. She might not realize, at first, that the computers had been off-line the day Candy had shown up on DCF's doorstep. Or that, thanks to the yellow notebook now resting in the bottom of Sarah's box, the new computer system contained not one word of information about James Tyrone Parker.

Sarah refused to fool herself into thinking Connie

would forget about the boy. At best, taking the notepad bought her some time. A few days to convince Ty to keep Jimmy on the Circle P until she found a legal way around her boss's decision. Given his reaction to The Glades, he wouldn't allow Jimmy to go there, would he?

She hoped not, but from the way things had gone lately, she couldn't guarantee it. Forty-eight hours ago she'd had the world on a string. A man she loved. A boy she adored. A business plan that might not make her rich, but would certainly give a deserving little boy all the good things life had to offer—home, family, education. In less than two days' time, she'd lost it all. Turning, Sarah trudged to her car.

THE DRIVE INTO FORT PIERCE stretched interminably. Ranches, dairy farms and orange groves blurred past while Ty marshaled his thoughts. On the outskirts of town, he swung by the jeweler's his family had used for four generations. By the time he made the final turn into Sarah's neighborhood, he had a ring in his pocket, knots in his stomach and a plan to show her how much he'd changed.

And if that doesn't work?

Ty prayed it wouldn't come to that.

Of course, putting his plan to work required talking with Sarah. Which was kind of hard to do when her car wasn't in the driveway and no one answered his knock at the door.

His breath stalled. Was he too late? Had she already arranged for Jimmy's transfer into the system?

Like he'd let that happen.

Just the thought of the little tyke bouncing from one foster home to another nearly made him sick to his stomach. He lifted Sarah's duffel bag from his truck and placed it on her front porch next to a plant that hadn't survived the freeze.

Minutes later, her car pulled into the driveway.

Knowing he'd have one chance to win her heart, Ty braced himself. He waited, hoping Sarah would race from her car and into his arms, fearing she'd storm across the lawn, demanding he immediately turn Jimmy over to her.

Instead, she simply sat. Her hands clenched on the steering wheel, she stared.

Long seconds passed.

Something twisted in Ty's gut as he studied Sarah's ashen face. When she finally broke the connection, he noted defeat in her rounded shoulders and the slow steps she took to the rear of her car. He swallowed, watching as she wrestled a bulky cardboard box from the trunk. He'd carried one similarly loaded when he left Jackson Cole, and knew her time at the DCF had ended.

For someone who'd left a stressful job to start a new life, Sarah didn't look happy. In fact, he'd never seen her so dispirited. An urge to go to her aid stirred in his chest, but this was not the Circle P. There were no rattlesnakes to guard against. He couldn't rescue her from stampeding cattle. With no clear-cut enemy to fight, he settled for taking the heavy box from her arms.

Sarah refused to meet his eyes. She scanned the yard, the porch, the air beside him before her gaze came to rest at his feet.

"Where's Jimmy?" she asked quietly.

"Seth and Doris have him. You and I need to talk. It's not the kind of conversation we can have anywhere near that little pitcher with big ears."

His description of Jimmy brought a wobbly smile

to the lips Ty craved to kiss. He held back, knowing Sarah needed time to gather her wits for the hard discussion ahead of them.

At last she sighed. “You’ve come this far. You might as well come inside.”

“That’s not exactly the warm welcome I was hoping for,” he mumbled.

“Best I can do at the moment,” she said.

Though she hadn’t said she was glad to see him, he took it as a good sign when she made quick work of opening the door. She pointed to a low table. “Make yourself at home. I’ll be right back,” she whispered before disappearing down the hall.

Ty placed the box on the table. After retrieving the rest of her things from the porch, he took his first look at her house. An open floor plan created a sense of spaciousness and drew his focus to the backyard.

He sucked in a breath. Browned and dying vegetation filled the view through wall-to-wall glass sliders. He moved to the patio, bending down to poke and prod at blackened leaves in one of the planters. Gently, ever so gently, he scraped the soil away until he exposed the roots of one orchid, then another.

“Ty?” Sarah called from the living room.

“Out here.” He slipped his pocketknife back into its case. When Sarah stepped onto the porch in jeans and a plain white T-shirt that showcased her curvy figure, he swallowed. Dusting the dirt from hands he wanted to wrap around her, he focused on her flowers.

“I saw what was left of a plant out front. Did the freeze take everything?”

“All of them.” She nodded, her pale face whitening. “Every single orchid. All the plumeria. There’s nothing left.”

Ty fought the urge to stand and wipe the glistening tears from Sarah's cheeks. She hadn't given any indication that she wanted a shoulder to lean on. And certainly not his. Not knowing what else to do, he flexed his fingers.

"I'm more of a rancher than a farmer," he said at last. "But this root stock looks okay. It might come back if it's cared for proper."

Sarah leaned in so close he caught a whiff of her perfume. The first spark of life glinted in her pain-filled eyes. "Really?"

"Maybe." Thinking straight when Sarah was within arm's reach wasn't the easiest thing he'd ever done. He drew back until her scent no longer demanded he put his arms around her and pull her close. Her flowers… he had to keep the focus on her flowers. "I've seen plants on the ranch that looked a lot like this. You'll lose some—no way around that—but maybe…"

"Thanks," she whispered.

Ty saw the hopeful look she gave the mottled leaves, noted the way she rubbed her fingers together. If he hadn't been standing there, he had no doubt she'd be up to her elbows in potting soil. "I can help you with these later," he offered, hoping she still wanted him around after they talked.

Her weight shifted from one foot to another. "We'll see," she said before leading the way back inside. In the living room, she eyed the letter he'd strategically placed on the kitchen counter. "So…" She paused for a breath that sounded anything but steady. "You know."

"Yeah." She didn't need to explain. They both knew she was talking about Jimmy. Ty aimed for nonchalance and failed. "Why didn't you tell me?"

"And what? Hear you say 'I told you so'?" Sarah's

fists landed at her trim waist. "You'd said all along he wasn't yours. Couldn't be." Her mouth twisted. "I guess, you were right."

"That still doesn't explain why you left without telling me," he said, struggling for calm and missing it by a hair. This wasn't the conversation he'd planned on, the one where they professed their love for one another and wound up in each other's arms. "I wish you'd come to me."

"You forget I was there for all your blood-is-everything lectures."

She'd misjudged him, something he couldn't let slide. "This from the person who believes environment trumps nature? You didn't even stop to consider that I might have changed."

He *had* changed. He'd left Jimmy at the Circle P instead of parking him on the DCF's doorstep. He'd hung the boy's picture in the family gallery. He'd even called his friend Dave, taken steps to ensure the boy's future.

Sarah acted as if she hadn't heard a word he'd said. She stalked across the room. "I knew you'd send him back. I wanted to give you an out that wouldn't tie you to…to Jimmy." Her lips wobbled. "To me. I tried to adopt him…."

Her words petered out as if she'd finally realized what he'd said. Her eyes narrowed in on him. "What do you mean, you changed?"

"People change." Far more interested in hearing her side of the story than telling his, Ty lifted his chin. "You said you tried. What happened?"

Sarah's bravado collapsed. "I've lost everything. To get custody of Jimmy, I had to quit my job. Then, my boss refused to process my custody application. Talk about irony."

Anger burned Ty's throat as Sarah described the confrontation with her ex-boss. A growl formed deep in his chest when he heard Connie thought a few weeks in a group home would be good for the boy. The only way Jimmy would ever set foot into The Glades was over his dead body.

But he'd like to see the woman try.

According to Dave, putting Ty's name on Jimmy's birth certificate had been the only smart move Millie had made after leaving the Circle P. One smart move was all it took, though. That one act bound Jimmy to him forever. It also protected the boy from misguided social workers who had their own personal axes to grind.

"You don't have to worry about Connie anymore."

Something bordering on panic flickered in Sarah's eyes. Ty looked down at the slim fingers on his sleeve and wondered when she'd reached out to him.

"Please, Ty. I'll never ask for anything else from you if you'll only keep him on the Circle P until I get this mess straightened out. There has to be a way. I'll find it."

"No." Ty held up his hand, signaling her to a stop. "No, that's not going to happen."

Sarah blinked in obvious confusion.

"I know I don't have a job." She gestured to what was left of her garden. "I don't even have much of a business plan. But I have savings. This house. If it takes every dime, I *will* find a way—"

"No," he interrupted. Unable to bear her pleas and unwilling to let her go on, Ty grasped Sarah's elbows. "Jimmy already has a home. With me. That's part of what I meant when I said I'd changed." He'd gone from simply wanting to give the orphan an experience to remember on the cattle drive, to the point where he couldn't imagine life without the little boy at his side.

"Despite the test results?" Sarah challenged.

How he felt about the boy was one thing. Putting it into words was something else. "It's the right thing to do," he said simply.

Dissatisfaction showed in the firm set of Sarah's lips. "That's not enough."

When she tried to pull away, Ty held fast. "Look, I love the little tyke, okay? I spoke to an attorney friend of mine. Bottom line—I'm legally Jimmy's dad, no matter what."

"And if his biological father…?" Sarah started.

Ty shook his head. "There's not much chance of that happening."

Relinquishing his hold on her, he retreated. With his back against the wall, he told her about the discovery he'd made while they were hanging Jimmy's picture. "If anyone ever needs to know, J.D.'s trunk is in the attic. His hairbrush, toothbrush, clothes—it's all in there. We'll have plenty of DNA if the time comes that we ever need it."

She stared at him, incredulous. "Your wife and your best friend? And yet…" She moistened her lips. "You love him?"

"Like the son I've always wanted."

He watched the fight seep out of her. Her shoulders slumped. A wavering smile replaced the frown she'd worn. So far, they'd spent a lot of time talking about Jimmy. But the child wasn't the only reason he'd come to Fort Pierce. Not even the main reason. No, his purpose for being there stood in front of him looking for all the world as if she'd lost her best friend. He resisted the urge to cross the room and sweep her into his arms.

He'd come this far, but he couldn't go any farther without some sign on her part to let him know they still wanted the same things.

"Look, I know you've lost a lot—your job, the business you'd planned to start—but you haven't lost everything. You've still got me—and Jimmy—if you want us."

"More than you'll ever know," she whispered.

This time there was no mistaking the flare of hope in Sarah's eyes. For the first time since he'd read the DNA report, some of the tension bled off Ty's shoulders. Managing a smile, he let his eyes drink their fill. From her red curls to her pert nose, her big heart to her stubborn determination, he loved her more than he'd ever loved anyone in his life…or ever would.

He cleared his throat. In a voice that was surprisingly steady for a man whose knees were knocking, he said, "Raising a kid's not like raising cattle. They need more TLC. It's too big a job for one man. What do you say we do it together?"

Sarah met his gaze head-on. "Are you asking me to be the mother of your child? Or to be your wife?"

She'd never been one to let him slide on the important matters. It was just one of many things he loved about her. Fumbling for the dainty piece of jewelry he'd slipped into his pocket on the way to her house, he went down on one knee.

His heart pounded in his throat as he took her hand in his and said the words men were supposed to say to the women who made their lives complete. "Sarah Magarity, I love you with all my heart and soul. Will you make me the happiest man in the world? Will you marry me?"

Ty was sure he aged a decade in the second it took

Sarah to relieve him of his misery. Her soft "Yes. Oh, yes!" put all his fears to rest.

"Now, don't get too attached to this ring," he said, slipping the slim band with its simple solitaire onto her finger. "I have the jeweler on speed dial. He promised to stay open so we can come in and pick out one you'll wear forever."

"I think this one will do quite nicely." Sarah's gaze swung from the sparkle on her finger to his eyes. With a look that firmed his desire to make her his own, she said, "I love you, Ty Parker."

Then, they were in each other's arms, his lips on hers and hers on his, possessing each other, confirming their love for one another, promising forever. When they finally drew apart, Ty took a deep breath. The son he'd always wanted waited for them at the ranch while the woman of his dreams, his future, rested in the crook of his arm. He leaned in for another kiss to sustain him until they were home on the Circle P.

Epilogue

The sun had spread a pinkish glow against the dark horizon by the time Sarah toted two mugs of coffee from the kitchen to the great room. She paused in the doorway, her eyes sweeping over the garland strung with twinkling lights along the banister and stair rails. Hundreds of ornaments, most heirlooms handed down from one generation of Parkers to the next, dotted the enormous Christmas tree Ty had erected in one corner. A flood of gaily wrapped gifts spread out from under its tinsel-draped boughs. The bike she and Ty had spent the night assembling leaned proudly on its kickstand at the edge of the sea of presents. The view was a far cry from the Christmas she'd hastily cobbled together for Jimmy last year, and warmth flooded Sarah's chest.

She moved to where Ty sat on the couch.

"You ready for all this?" she asked.

"I think I'm more excited than he is," Ty chuckled, the fatigue of staying up all night hidden behind his wide smile.

When he reached for his cup, his fingers brushed hers, sending a shiver of longing through her. She saw the same deep emotions swimming in his dark brown eyes as she traced her fingers down his unshaven cheek.

Ty patted the seat beside him and she slid under his welcoming arm, her side pressed against his wide chest. His breath whispered through her hair. “You think he’ll like everything?”

“He’s a very lucky boy,” she said, knowing Jimmy would be thrilled. “I can’t wait to see his face when you tell him about Niceta.” Though the colt couldn’t be ridden for another couple of years, Jimmy’s riding lessons were coming along well enough that Ty had decided the boy was ready for the responsibility of having his own horse.

“And the rest, are you ready for that, too?” She twisted the rings on the third finger of her left hand.

Married.

Who would have thought she’d be married and the mother of a six-year-old by the time another Christmas rolled around? But, after a summer wedding ceremony in her parents’ backyard, they’d followed the advice of Ty’s friend and formalized her ties to Jimmy.

And they’d laid their last questions about the boy to rest. Together, she and Ty had braved the trunk upstairs where they’d collected hair samples from J.D.’s brush. Tests using blood the lab already had on file had confirmed Ty’s suspicions. Since J.D.’s parents were long gone, the paperwork had sailed through the courts, the final decree arriving in time for a truly memorable Thanksgiving. Even Connie hadn’t been able to stand in their way.

Ty’s big hand covered hers. “Lots of changes in the wind. How ’bout you? Any doubts?”

“Not a single one,” Sarah answered. She’d discovered true love, happiness and a new home on the Circle P.

“Good. ’Cause I’m really looking forward to our

honeymoon." He lifted her ring finger to his lips and brushed a kiss against it. "I can't wait to have you all to myself on some secluded beach in Hawaii. Makes me almost wish we weren't waiting till tomorrow to take off."

"You'd give up seeing Jimmy's face on Christmas morning?" she asked, pretending to be shocked. Their bags were already packed and by the front door. Tomorrow afternoon, she and Ty would leave Jimmy in Seth's and Doris's capable hands while they finally embarked on her Hawaiian vacation. Only, now that the trip was more than just a plant-buying expedition, Sarah thought it'd be a lot more fun. Her face warmed as she thought of two glorious weeks in a tropical paradise with the man of her dreams.

"Never," Ty murmured. "But you have to promise me we won't spend *all* our time traipsing from one flower nursery to another."

"Flowers? Who said anything about flowers?" she teased, though they both knew she needed to add to her stock. Thanks to Ty's advice, she'd salvaged nearly half her plants after last year's freeze. Once she'd established a website for Parker Plumeria, her fledgling nursery had more orders than it could fill.

"I wouldn't mind getting a head start on that honeymoon right now," Ty said, his hand cupping her shoulder.

Much as she wanted the same thing, the patter of feet on the floor overhead put an end to those thoughts. "Later," Sarah promised.

"Mom, Dad, it's Christmas! Did Santa Claus—" at the top of the stairs, a pajama-clad Jimmy stared down, his mouth a wide oval "—oh, wow!"

Moisture stung the corners of Sarah's eyes as the

boy—her son!—thundered down the stairs. Rising to sweep him into her arms, she dashed away her tears. Jimmy had started calling Ty his dad the weekend they'd stripped a floral print from the walls in one guest room and redecorated it with horses and cowboys. Another couple of months had passed when, after saying his prayers one night, Jimmy had asked if a boy could have two mothers.

For a second, Sarah's breath had frozen in her chest.

"Lots of kids have more than one mom," she'd assured him. "Ryan from your kindergarten class has two."

Jimmy had nodded solemnly. And from that moment on, she'd been his.

"Let's open presents," she suggested to the boy wiggling to peer around her.

"All right!"

An hour later, every carefully wrapped gift had been opened, examined and scattered throughout the room, and they'd gathered the ribbons and paper for recycling. While they munched on the orange rolls Doris had baked the night before, Sarah let her gaze sweep the room. A year ago, she'd faced the future as a single woman devoted to her job. But one little boy had changed her carefully scripted life and filled it with more joy than she'd been able to imagine. She'd taken a chance on love and been rewarded with the best it had to offer.

She caught Ty's eye. "I think it's time we showed Jimmy his other Christmas present, don't you?"

"There's more?" Jimmy asked, his eyes widening.

"One more." Ty smiled.

Outside, tropical flowers scented a warm winter breeze and the sun shone brightly against a blue sky.

From the barn, horses whinnied softly over the distant lowing of cattle. Her hand firmly in Ty's, Sarah's chest swelled with happiness as she headed toward the barn with the man she loved and their son.

* * * * *

Coming January 2013

THE OTHER SIDE OF US
A brand-new novel
from Harlequin® Superromance® author
Sarah Mayberry

In recovery from a serious accident, Mackenzie Williams is beating all the doctors' predictions. But she needs single-minded focus. She doesn't *need the distraction of neighbors—especially good-looking ones like Oliver Garrett!*

MACKENZIE BREATHED DEEPLY to recover from the workout. She'd pushed herself too far but she wanted to accelerate her rehabilitation. Still, she needed to lie down to combat the nausea and shaking muscles.

There was a knock on the front door. Who on earth would be visiting her on a Thursday morning? Probably a cold-calling salesperson.

She answered, but her pithy rejection died before she'd formed the first words.

The man on her doorstep was definitely not a cold caller. Nothing about this man was cold, from the auburn of his wavy hair to his brown eyes to his sensual mouth. Nothing cold about those broad shoulders, flat belly and lean hips, either.

"Hey," he said in a shiver-inducing baritone. "I'm Oliver Garrett. I moved in next door." His smile was so warm and vibrant it was almost offensive.

"Mackenzie Williams." Oh, no. Her legs were starting to

tremble, indicating they wouldn't hold up long. Any second now she would embarrass herself in front of this complete and very good-looking stranger.

"It's been years since I was down here." He seemed to settle in for a chat. "It doesn't look as though—"

"I have to go." Her stomach rolled as she shut the door. The last thing she registered was the look of shock on Oliver's face at her abrupt dismissal.

And somehow she knew their neighborly relations would be a lot cooler now.

Will Mackenzie be able to make it up to Oliver for her rude introduction?
Find out in THE OTHER SIDE OF US
by Sarah Mayberry, available January 2013 from Harlequin® Superromance®. PLUS, exciting changes are in the works! Enjoy the same great stories in a longer format and new look—beginning January 2013!

HSREXP1212HH

COMING NEXT MONTH
from Harlequin® American Romance®

AVAILABLE JANUARY 2, 2013

#1433 A CALLAHAN OUTLAW'S TWINS

Callahan Cowboys

Tina Leonard

When Kendall Phillips announces she is pregnant with Sloan Callahan's twin sons, the loner ex-military man realizes he has to change his outlaw ways...and start thinking of a way to propose!

#1434 REMEMBER ME, COWBOY

Coffee Creek, Montana

C.J. Carmichael

An accident left Corb Lambert with amnesia and he can't remember Laurel Sheridan, let alone getting her pregnant. Will a hasty marriage solve these problems—or make them worse?

#1435 THE SEAL'S VALENTINE

Operation: Family

Laura Marie Altom

Navy SEAL Tristan Bartoni's heart was broken when his wife left him and took their son. So how can he be attracted to Brynn Langtoine and risk his heart again for her and her cute kids?

#1436 HER RANCHER HERO

Saddlers Prairie

Ann Roth

Cody Naylor fosters four troubled boys on Hope Ranch. Is it appropriate that Cody is falling for his new housekeeper? Will her leaving at the end of the summer throw the boys into turmoil? Or just Cody?

Turn the page for a preview of

THE OTHER SIDE OF US

by

Sarah Mayberry,

coming January 2013
from Harlequin® Superromance®.

PLUS, exciting changes are in the works!
Enjoy the same great stories in a longer format
and new look—beginning January 2013!